A MIRROR OF SHALOTT

A Mirror of Shallot

*Tales of the Supernatural,
Told at a Symposium*

Robert Hugh Benson

CLUNY

Providence, Rhode Island

CLUNY EDITION, 2024

This Cluny edition is an unabridged republication of the
1912 Sir Isaac Pitman & Sons edition of *A Mirror of Shalott*.

AUTHOR'S NOTE:
*Most of the Stories in this volume have already appeared
in the* Ecclesiastical Review; *one of them in the* Catholic Fireside.
They are printed here by the kind permission of the Editors. (R. H. B.)

For information regarding this title
or any other Cluny Media publication,
please write to info@clunymedia.com, or to
Cluny Media, P.O. Box 1664, Providence, RI 02901

VISIT US ONLINE AT WWW.CLUNYMEDIA.COM

ISBN: 978-1685953515

Cover design by Clarke & Clarke
Cover images: Caspar David Friedrich,
The Cemetery Entrance, c. 1825, oil on canvas
Courtesy of Wikimedia Commons

CONTENTS

Primus est deorum cultus deos credere.

And moving through a mirror clear
That hangs before her all the year
Shadows of the world appear…

The Lady of Shalott

Prologue

"I maintain," said Monsignor with a brisk air of aggressiveness and holding his pipe a moment from his mouth, "I maintain that agnosticism is the only reasonable position in these matters. Your common agnostic is no agnostic at all; he is the most dogmatic of sectarians. He declares that such things do not happen, or that they can be explained always on a materialistic basis. Now your Catholic—"

Father Bianchi bristled, and rolled his black eyes fiercely. If he had had a moustache he would have twirled it.

We were sitting in the upstairs *sala* of the presbytery attached to the Canadian Church of S. Filippo in Rome. It had been a large comfortless room, stone-floored, stone-walled and plaster-ceilinged, but it had been made possible by numerous rugs, a number of armchairs and an English fireplace. Above, in the cold plaster, dingy flesh-coloured gods and nymphs attempted to lounge on cotton clouds with studied ease, looking down dispiritedly upon seven priests and myself, a layman, who sat in a shallow semicircle round the red logs. In '71 the house had fallen into secular hands, whence issued the gods and nymphs, but in '97 the Church had come by her own again, and had not yet banished Olympus. There was no need to annihilate the conquered.

In the centre sat the Father Rector, a placid old man, and round about him were the rest of us—Monsignor Maxwell, a French priest, an English, an Italian, a Canadian, a German and myself. This was five years ago. I do not know where these people are now; one I think is in heaven, two I should suppose in purgatory, four on earth. In spite of my feelings towards Padre Bianchi, I should assign him to purgatory. He made a good death two years later in the Naples epidemic.

We had begun at supper by discussing modern miracles. The second nocturn had furnished the text to the mouth of Monsignor, and we had passed on by natural channels to levitation, table-turning, family curses, ghosts and banshees. The Italian was sceptical and scornful. Such things in his opinion did not take place; he excepted only the incidents recorded in the lives of the saints. I did not mind his scepticism (that, after all, injures no one but the sceptic); but scorn and contumely is another matter, and I was glad that Canon Maxwell had taken him in hand, for that priest has a shrewd and acrid tongue, and wears purple, besides, round his person and on his buttons, so he speaks with authority.

"You have some tale then, no doubt, Monsignor?" sneered the Italian.

The Englishman smiled with tight lips.

"Every one has," he said briefly. "Even you, Padre Bianchi, if you will but tell it."

The other shook his head indulgently.

"I will swear," he said, "that none here has such a tale at first-hand."

It was Father Meuron's turn to bristle.

"But yes!" he exclaimed.

Canon Maxwell drew on his pipe a moment or two and regarded the fire.

"I have a proposition to make," he said. "Father Bianchi is right. I have one tale, and Father Meuron has another. With the Father Rector's permission we will tell our tales, one each night. On Sunday two or three of us are supping at the French College, so that shall be holiday, and by Monday night these other gentlemen will, no doubt, have remembered experiences—even Father Bianchi, I believe. And Mr. Benson shall write them down, if he wishes to, and make an honest penny or two if he can get any publisher to take the book."

I hastened to express my approval of the scheme.

The Father Rector moved in his chair.

"That will be very amusing, Monsignor. I am entirely in favour of it, though I doubt my own capacity. I propose that Canon Maxwell takes the chair."

"Then I understand that all will contribute one story," said Monsignor briskly, "on those terms—"

There was a chorus of assent.

"One moment, Monsignor," interrupted Father Brent. "Would it not be worth while to have a short discussion first as to the whole affair? I must confess that my own ideas are not clear."

"Well," said Monsignor shortly, "on what point?"

The younger priest mused a moment.

"It is like this," he said. "Half at least of the stories one hears have no point—no reason. Take the ordinary haunted house tale, or the appearances at the time of death. Now what is the good of all that? They tell us nothing; they don't generally ask for prayers. It is just a white woman wringing her hands, or a groaning, or something. At the best one only finds a skeleton behind the panelling. Now my story, if I tell it, has absolutely no point at all."

"No point!" said Monsignor. "You mean that you don't understand the point, or that no one does? Is that it?"

"Well, yes; but there is more too. How do you square these things with purgatory? How can spirits go wandering about, and be so futile at the end of it too? Then why is everything so vague? Why don't they give us a hint— I'm not wanting precise information—but a kind of hint of the way things go? Then the whole thing is mixed up with such childish nonsense. Look at the spiritualists, and the tambourine business, and table-rapping. Either those things are true, even if they're diabolical—and in that case people in the spiritual world seem considerably sillier even than people in this—or they're not true; and in that case the whole thing is so fraudulent that it seems useless to inquire. Do you see my point?"

"I see about twenty," said Monsignor. "And it would take all night to answer them. But let me take two. Firstly, I am entirely willing to allow that half the stories one hears are fraudulent or hysterical; I'm quite ready to allow that. But it seems to me that there remain a good many others; and if one doesn't accept those to some extent, I don't know what becomes of the value of human evidence. Now one of your points, I take it, is that even these seem generally quite pointless and useless? Is that it?"

"More or less," said Father Brent.

"Well, first, I would say this. It seems perfectly clear that these other stories aren't sent to help our faith, or anything like that. I don't believe that for one instant. We have got all we need in the Catholic Church, and the moral witness, and the rest. But what I don't understand in your position is this—What earthly right have you got to think that they're sent just for your benefit?"

The other demurred.

"I don't," he said. "But I suppose they're sent for somebody's benefit."

"Somebody still on earth, you mean?"

"Well—yes."

Monsignor leaned forward.

"My dear Father, how very provincial you are—if I may say so! Here is this exceedingly small earth, certainly with a very fair number of people living on it—but absolutely a mere fraction of the number of intelligences that are in existence. And all about us—since we must use that phrase—is a spiritual world, compared with which the present generation is as a family of ants in the middle of London. Things happen—this spiritual world is crammed full of energy and movement and affairs.… We know practically nothing of it all, except those few main principles which are called the Catholic Faith—nothing else. What conceivable right have we to demand that the little glimpses that we seem to get sometimes of the spiritual world are given us for our benefit or information?"

"Then why are they given?"

Monsignor made a disdainful sound with closed lips.

"My dear Father, a boy drops a piece of orange peel into the middle of the ants' nest one day. The ants summon a council at once and sit on it. They discuss the lesson that is to be learned from the orange peel: they come to the conclusion that Buckingham Palace must be built entirely of orange peel, and that the reason why it was sent to them was that they were to learn that great and important lesson."

Father Brent sat up suddenly.

"My dear Monsignor, you seem to me to strike at the root of revelation. If we aren't to deduce things from supernatural incidents, why should we believe in our religion?"

Monsignor lifted a hand.

"Next day there is slid into the ants' nest a box divided into compartments, containing exactly that which the ants need for the winter, food and so forth. The ants hold another parliament. Two-thirds of them who have determined in the last hour or two to reject the Buckingham Palace-orange peel theory, reject this too. All is fortuitous, they say. The orange peel was; therefore the box is!"

Father Brent relapsed, smiling.

"That is all right," he said. "I was a fool."

"One-third," continued the Canon severely, "came to the not unreasonable conclusion that a box which shows such evident signs of intelligence, and of knowledge and care for their circumstances, proceeds from an Intelligence which wishes them well. But there is a further schism. Half of those who accept revelation remain agnostic about most other things, and say frankly that they don't know—especially as regards the orange peel. The other half rages on about the orange peel; some are inclined to think that there was no orange peel—it was no more than an hallucination. Others think that there is some remarkable lesson to be learnt from it, and these differ violently as to what the lesson is. Others, again, regard it unintelligently and say to one another, 'Look. A piece of orange peel! How very beautiful and important.'"

(I laughed softly to myself. Monsignor spoke with such earnestness. I would like him to be my advocate if I ever get into trouble.)

"And, my dear Father," he went on, "I take up the first position of those who accept revelation, and I acknowledge the fact of the orange peel; but really nothing more. My religion teaches me that there is a spiritual world of indefinite size, and that things not only may, but must, go on there which have nothing particular to do with me. Every now and then I get a glimpse of some of these things— an orange pip, at the very least. But I don't immediately demand an explanation. It probably isn't deliberately meant for me at all. It has something to do with affairs of which I know nothing, and which manage to get on quite well without me."

Father Brent, still smiling, protested once more.

"Very ingenious, Monsignor; but then why does it happen to happen to you?"

"I have not the slightest idea, any more than I have the slightest idea why Providence made me break a tooth this morning. I accept the fact; I believe that somehow it works into the scheme. But I do not for that reason claim to understand it…. And as for purgatory—well, I ask you,

What in the world do we know about purgatory except that there is such a thing, and that the souls of the faithful there detained are assisted by our suffrages? What conceivable possibility is there that we should understand the details of its management? My dear Father, no one in this world has a greater respect for, or confidence in, dogmatic theology than myself; in fact, I may say that it is the only thing which I do have confidence in. But I respect the limits which it itself has laid down."

"Then you are an agnostic as regards everything but the faith?"

"Certainly I am.—Well, possibly except mathematics, too, and so is any wise man. I have my ideas, of course, and I make guesses sometimes; but I really do not think that they have any value."

There was silence a moment.

"Then there is this, too," he continued. "It really is important to remember that the spiritual world exists in another mode from that in which the material world exists. That is where the ant-simile breaks down. It is more as if an ant went to the Royal Academy.... Of course in the faith we have an adequate and guaranteed translation of the supernatural into the natural, and vice versâ; and in these ghost stories, or whatever we call them, we have a certain sort of translation too. The Real Thing, whatever it is, expresses itself in material terms, more or less. But in these we have no sort of guarantee that the translation is adequate, or that we are adequate to understand it. We can try, of course; but we really don't know. Therefore it seems to me that in all ghost stories the best thing is to hear it, to satisfy ourselves that the evidence is good or bad, and then to hold our tongues. We don't want elaborate commentaries on what may be, after all, an utterly corrupt text."

"But some of them do support the faith," put in Father Brent.

"So much the better then. But it is much safer not to lean your weight on them. You never can tell. Now with the faith you can."

There was another silence.

Then the Rector stood up smiling.

"Night prayers, Reverend Fathers," he said.

I

Monsignor Maxwell's Tale

I was still thinking over the Canon's remarks as I came up into the *sala* on the following evening. They seemed to me eminently sensible; or, in other words, they exactly represented what I had always held myself, though I had never so expressed them even to my own mind.

I felt some interest, therefore, in the question as to the class to which Monsignor's own story would be found to belong—whether to that which contains merely a series of phenomena, or to that which appeared to corroborate the Christian religion.

The rest of the company, with two or three strangers, were already in their places when I arrived; and Monsignor was enthroned in the centre chair, staring with a preoccupied look at the blazing fire. The Rector was on his right.

The conversation died away at last; there was a shifting of attitudes. Then the Canon looked at his watch, bending his sleek grey head sideways.

"We have twenty minutes," he said in his terse way. Then he crossed his buckled feet and began without any preliminary comment.

"This happened to me in England. Naturally I shall not mention where it took place, nor how long ago.

"I knew a man, a Catholic from birth, of a remarkable

faith and piety. He had tried his vocation in religion again and again, for he seemed a born religious; but his health had always broken down, and he had finally married. He had been told by his director that his vocation was evidently to live in the world, and as a layman. Whether I agree or disagree with the latter part of his advice is not to the point, but there was no question as to the former part of it. The man's health simply could not stand it. But he led a most mortified and interior life with his wife in his London house, with a servant or two to look after them, and was present daily at mass at the church that I served then. His wife, too, was a very exceptional woman, utterly devoted to her husband, and I may say that I never paid them a visit without being very much the better for it.

"Now he had a brother, a solicitor in a town in the north, also a Catholic, of course, whom I never saw, but who enters very materially into the story. We will call the brothers, if you please, Mr. James and Mr. Herbert, though I need not say that these were not their names.

"One morning after mass Mr. James came to me in the sacristy and said he wished to have a word with me, so I took him through into the presbytery and up into my own room. I could see that something was very much the matter with him.

"He took a letter out and gave it me to read. It was from his brother—Mr. Herbert—and contained very sad news indeed—nothing else, in fact, than an announcement of his intention to secede from the Church. There was a story of a marriage difficulty, too, as there so often is in such cases. He had fallen in love with a woman of strong agnostic convictions, and nothing would induce her to marry him unless he conformed to her religion—such as it was. But, to do Mr. Herbert justice, I could see that there was a real loss of faith as well. There were two or three sheets filled with arguments that I could see were real to the man—or statements, perhaps, rather than arguments—against the Incarnation and the inspiration of the Scriptures, and the authority of the Church, and so on, and I must confess that they were not mere clap-trap. The woman was plainly capable and shrewd and had been talking to him, and both his heart and his head were seriously entangled.

"Well, I handed the letter back to Mr. James, and said what I could, recommended a book or two, promised to get him prayers, and so on, but the man waved it aside.

"'Yes, yes, Father,' he said, 'I know, and I thank you, but I must do more than that. You don't know what this means to me. I got the letter yesterday at midday, and I may say that I have done nothing but pray since, and this morning at mass I saw a light—at least, I think so, and I want your advice.'

"He was terribly excited, his eyes were bright, and the lines in his face deeper than I had ever seen them, (for he was only just entering middle age,) and the papers shook in his hands. I did my best to quiet him, but it was no good. All his tranquillity, which had been one of his most striking virtues, was gone, and I could see that his whole being was rent.

"'You don't know what this means to me, he said again. 'There is only one thing to be done. I must offer myself for him.'

"Well, I didn't understand him at first, but we talked a little, and at last I found that the idea of mystical substitution had seized on his mind. He was persuaded that he must make an offering of himself to God, and ask to be allowed to bear the temptation instead of his brother. Of course we know that that is one of the claims of the contemplative, but, to tell the truth, I had never come across it before in my own experience.

"Well, he didn't want my opinion upon the doctrine, and, indeed, I was glad he didn't, for I knew nothing about it myself, but he wanted to know if I thought him justified in running the risk—for he seemed to take it as a matter of course that I believed it.

"'Am I strong enough, Father?' he asked. 'Can I bear it? I cannot imagine my losing my faith,' and a smile just flickered on his mouth and vanished again in trembling, 'but—but God knows how weak I am.'

"Well, I reassured him on that point, at any rate, and told him that, so far as his faith was concerned, I considered it robust enough. To tell the truth, I suppose I was a little careless, because—because—" and Monsignor shifted a little in his chair and looked round. "Well, it was all so bewildering.

"Well, he soon went after that, saying that he would tell his wife, and imploring me to get prayers for him in his struggle, and I was left alone to think it over.

"For the next day or two he appeared at mass as usual, and just waited for me one morning to tell me that he had made the offering of himself before God. Then I had to go into the country on some business or other, and was away from Monday to Saturday.

"Now to tell the truth I did not think of him very much; I was harassed and bothered myself, about my business, and scarcely did more than just mention his name at the altar, and I am ashamed to say I completely forgot to get prayers elsewhere for his brother or himself, and I was entirely unprepared for what was waiting for me when I reached home on the Saturday evening."

Monsignor paused a moment or two. He was evidently speaking with a certain difficulty. His brisk business-like way of talking had just a tinge of feeling in it which it generally lacked, and he moved in his chair now and then with something almost like nervousness. The other priests were silent. The young Englishman was bending forward in the firelight with his chin on his hands, and old Father Stein had sat back in his chair very quiet and was shading his face from the candlelight.

"My housekeeper heard my key in the lock of the front door," went on Canon Maxwell, "and was waiting for me in the hall. She told me that Mr. James' wife had sent round four times for me that afternoon, saying she must have me at once on my return, and that any delay might be fatal. But it was not a case for the Last Sacraments, apparently. I was astonished by such phrases, but they were evidently word for word what she had said, for my housekeeper apologized for repeating them.

"'There is something terribly the matter, Father,' she said; 'the last time the servant was crying, and said that her master was out of his mind.'

"Well, I ran into church and told my penitents there

that they must wait, or go to my colleague, and that I had had a sick-call and did not know how long I should be away; and then I ran straight out of the church, and down to the house which was three or four streets off. (You must forgive my telling you this story with so many details, but somehow it is the only way I can do it; it is all as vivid and clear as if it had happened last week....)

"It was a November evening; all the lamps were lit as I passed out of the thoroughfare down the side-road where his house was; here the pavements were empty, and I ran again as fast as I could down the street and up the steps that led to his front door. Even as I stood there out of breath, I knew that something was seriously wrong.

"Down in the kitchen below, as I could see plain-ly through the lighted windows, the Irish cook had been kneeling with her face hidden on the table; and she was now staring up at me with her eyes red and her hair disor-dered, as the peal of the bell died away. Then she was out in the area almost screaming—

"'Oh, God bless you, Father!' and then the door opened, and I was in the hall.

"'Where is he?' I asked the maid, all panting with my run, and she told me, in his study, and then I was up at the door in a moment, knocking, and then, without waiting, I went in.

"It was one of those little back rooms that you see sometimes in London houses, just at the top of the stairs that lead down to the servants' quarters. There was a little garden at the back of the house and a side street beyond that. The curtains over the window had not been drawn, and a lamp shone into the room from the lane outside. But I did not understand that at the time. I was only aware that the room was dark, except for a pale light that lay across the floor and wall and on the door that I closed behind me.

"But the horror of the room was beyond anything that I have ever felt. It—it—"

Monsignor hesitated. "It was almost physical, and yet I knew it was not, but it was the sense of some extraordinary influence, spiritual and on the point of—" he stopped again. "You must forgive me," he said, "but I can put it in no way but this—it seemed on the point of expressing itself visibly or tangibly; at any rate I felt my hair rise slowly as I stood there, and then I leaned back against the door and groped for the handle."

Old Father Stein nodded gravely.

"I know, I know," he said in his heavy voice; "it was so with me at Benares."

"It was so dark at first," went on Monsignor, "that I could see nothing but the outlines of the furniture. There was the writing table and so on immediately on my left, the fireplace beyond it in the left-hand wall; a tall bureau beside the window, opposite me. Then I felt my hand seized and gripped in the dark, and I looked down, horribly startled, and saw that his wife had been kneeling at his *prie-dieu* on the right, and had turned and clutched my hand, as she saw me in the light of the street-lamp; but she said nothing, and her silence was the worst of all.

"I looked again round the room and then suddenly gasped, and I must confess, nearly screamed, because, quite close to me, the man sat and stared up at me. I had been confused as I came in, and I believe now that I only had not seen him, because I had taken the dark outline of his body, and the whiteness of his face, to be a little side-table with papers upon it, that often stood by his writing-place.

"Well, however that was, here was the man, quite close to me, sitting bolt upright with the lamplight falling on that deadly face, all lined as it was, with patches of dark beneath those awful bright eyes."

Monsignor stopped again, and I could see that the hand on his chair-arm twitched sharply once or twice.

"Well, two or three times, I should think, I opened my mouth to speak, and I have never known before or since what it was, literally, not to be able to do it. It was as if a hand gripped my throat each time. I suppose it was a kind of hysterical contraction of the muscles. I understood then why the wife could not speak. The only emotion I was conscious of was an insane desire to get out of the room and the house, away from that terrifying silence and oppressiveness and, under God, I believe that the one thing that kept me there was that frightful grip on my fingers, that tightened, as if the wife read my thoughts, even as the desire surged up.

"I stood there, I suppose, half a minute more before I moved or spoke, and then I made a little, motion, and drew my fingers out of hers, and made the sign of the cross, and even then I dared not speak. But the face remained still in that tense quietness, and the bright sunken eyes never flinched or stirred.

"Then I dropped on my knees; and at last, with really an extraordinary effort, as if I was breaking something, I managed to speak and say a prayer or two, the *Our Father* and the *Hail Mary*—I could remember nothing else. Then I glanced at him quickly, and he had not stirred, but was watching me with a kind of bitter indifference—that is all I can say of it. I went on with the creed, finished it, said Amen, and then one loud harsh bark of laughter broke from him, and—and—I could swear that something else laughed too—"

A sharp exclamation broke from Father Brent, and a kind of sigh from the French priest, as Monsignor suddenly sat up and struck his hand on his knee at his last word, and my own heart leapt and stood still, while my nerves jangled like struck wires.

"There, there," said the Rector, "our nerves are out of order; be kind to us, Monsignor."

He shook his head.

"But I must tell you," he said, "though I hardly know what words to use.… This other laughter was not like his. I could not swear that—that there was a vibration of sound. It might have been interior, but it was there; it was objective and external to me…only I was absolutely convinced that there was laughter, neither mine, nor the man's, nor his wife's. There—that is all I can say of it."

He paused a moment.

"Well," he went on, "we got him upstairs at last, and on his bed. I tell you it was a very odd relief to get out of the room downstairs. He had not slept, his wife whispered to me as we went up, for four nights, not since the Monday in fact, and had scarcely eaten either. There was no time to hear more, for he turned round as he walked up and looked at us as we held him, and there was no more talking, with that face before us. And there we sat beside him in his bed-room—he lay quiet with closed eyes—and I did not dare to leave him till three or four in the morning, when I was nearly dead with weariness. His wife made me go then, and promised to send again if there was any change.

"Well, during the sung mass, at which I was not offici-ating, the message came, and I was back at his house direct-ly. There had been a change; he was now willing to talk. He looked ghastly, but his wife told me that she thought he had slept an hour or two, after I had left.

"Well, we talked, and I found that the man's faith was gone or, perhaps it is safer to say, completely obscured. I scarcely know how to express it, but if was as if he had practically no conception of what I was talking about.

"'I believed it once,' he said, 'yes, I am sure I did, but I can't imagine why or how.'

"'Then what is all this trouble of mind about?' I asked.

"'Why,' he said, 'why; if it is not true, what is left?'

"I didn't quite see what he meant, and asked him.

"'You,' he said, and just touched me with his finger, 'you and I,' and he touched himself, 'and—and—all this,' and he tapped the table, 'and—all that,' and he flung his arm out towards the window and the chimney pots and the bustling thoroughfare. 'All of it—all of it—what does it all mean, what is the good of it?'

"It was a piteous thing to see his face, the blackness and the misery of his despair at an empty meaningless world and a self that could do nothing but writhe and cry in the dark.

"You see the whole thing for him stood or fell by God, lived and moved in Him; now God was gone, and what was left?

"Well, of course I reminded him of his offering of himself to God for his brother. God had accepted it, I told him; and he just laughed miserably in my face.

"'Do you think Herbert suffered like this?' he asked.

"Well, I was tired and bewildered, and this seemed to me an answer. Of course you all see the explanation."

"The other suffered less because his faith was less," put in Father Brent instantly.

"Exactly," said Monsignor, "well, I am ashamed to say I didn't see that, at least not clearly enough to put it to him; but I did point out that it was of the very essence of his contract that he should suffer severely in the very manner in which he was suffering, and that the coincidence was remarkable, and, further, that the fact that he was in such distress, shewed that God was something to him after all. I don't know even then that I accepted the whole thing as being quite real. But what else could I say? … Well, he smiled again at that.

"'Have you never regretted a happy dream?' he said.

"Well, I am wearying you," said Monsignor, looking at his watch, "but I am just at the end. I went to that man every day for, I suppose, two or three hours for five or six weeks, and it seemed practically useless. I had never realized before so completely that faith was a gift which can be given or withdrawn; that it is something infused into us, not produced by us. Finally the man died of congestion of the brain."

"Good Lord!" said a voice.

"Yes," said Canon Maxwell, blowing down his pipe, "those—those were my sentiments."

"Monsignor! Do you mean he died without faith?"

"Father Jenks, I gave him the sacraments. He asked for them. I did not press too many questions; I thought it best to leave well alone."

"And the brother?"

"Oh, the brother—Mr. Herbert—was at the funeral, and informed me that the marriage was broken off, and I never heard of his apostacy. And there was one other person who contributed to the interest of the whole affair, and that was the wife."

"What happened to her?"

"She became a Poor Clare. She told me that self-immolation was the only possible act for her after what she had seen and known."

There was a long silence.

"Well, well, well," said Father Bianchi.

II

Father Meuron's Tale

FATHER Meuron was very voluble at supper on the Saturday. He exclaimed; he threw out his hands; his bright black eyes shone above his rosy cheeks; and his hair appeared to stand more on end than I had ever known it.

He sat at the farther side of the horse-shoe table from myself, and I was able to remark on his gaiety to the English priest who sat beside me, without fear of being overheard.

Father Brent smiled.

"He is drunk with *la gloire*," he said. "He is to tell the story tonight."

This explained everything.

I did not look forward, however, to his recital. I was confident that it would be full of tinsel and swooning maidens who ended their days in convents under Father Meuron's spiritual direction; and when he came upstairs I found a shadowy corner, a little back from the semi-circle, where I could fall asleep, if I wished, without provoking remark.

In fact I was totally unprepared for the character of his narrative.

When we had all taken our places and Monsignor's pipe was properly alight, and himself at full length in his deck-chair, the Frenchman began. He told his story in his own language; but I am venturing to render it in English as nearly as I am able.

"My contribution to the histories," he began, seated in his upright arm-chair in the centre of the circle, a little turned away from me, "my contribution to the histories which these good priests are to recite, is an affair of exorcism. That is a matter with which we who live in Europe are not familiar in these days. It would seem, I suppose, that grace has a certain power, accumulating through the centuries, of saturating even physical objects with its force. However men may rebel, yet the sacrifices offered and the prayers poured out have a faculty of holding Satan in check, and preventing his more formidable manifestations. Even in my own poor country at this hour, in spite of widespread apostasy, in spite even of the deliberate worship of Satan, yet grace is in the air; and it is seldom, indeed, that a priest has to deal with a case of possession. In your respectable England, too, it is the same; the simple piety of Protestants has kept alive to some extent the force of the Gospel. Here in this country it is somewhat different. The old powers have survived the Christian assault, and while they cannot live in holy Rome, there are corners where they do so." From my place I saw Padre Bianchi turn a furtive eye upon the speaker, and I thought I read in it an unwilling assent.

"However," went on the Frenchman, with a superb dismissory gesture, "my recital does not concern this continent, but the little island of La Souffrière. There circumstances are other than here. It was a stronghold of darkness when I was there in '91. Grace, while laying hold of men's hearts, had not yet penetrated the lower creation. Do you understand me? There were many holy persons whom I knew, who frequented the Sacraments and lived devoutly, but there were many of another manner. The ancient rites survived secretly amongst the negroes, and darkness—how shall I say it?—dimness made itself visible.

"However, to our history—"

The priest resettled himself in his chair and laid his fingers together like precious instruments.

He was enjoying himself vastly, and I could see that he was preparing himself for a revelation.

"It was in '91," he repeated, "that I went there with another of our Fathers to the mission-house. I will not trouble you, gentlemen, with recounting the tale of our arrival, nor of the months that followed it, except perhaps to tell you that I was astonished by much that I saw. Never until that time had I seen the power of the Sacraments so evident. In civilized lands, as I have suggested to you, the air is charged with grace. Each is no more than a wave in the deep sea. He who is without God's favour is not without His grace at each breath he draws. There are churches, religious, pious persons about him; there are centuries of prayers behind him. The very buildings he enters, as M. Huysmans has explained to us, are browned by prayer. Though a wicked child, he is yet in his Father's house: and the return from death to life is not such a crossing of the abyss, after all. But there in La Souffrière all is either divine or satanic, black or white, Christian or devilish. One stands as it were on the sea shore to watch the breakers of grace; and each is a miracle. I tell you I have seen holy catechumens foam at the mouth and roll their eyes in pain, as the saving water fell on them, and that which was within went out. As the Gospel relates, '*Spiritus conturbavit illum: et elisus in terram, volutabatur spumans.*'"

Father Meuron paused again. I was interested to hear this corroboration of evidence that had come before me on other occasions. More than one missionary had told me the same thing; and I had found in their tales a parallel to those related by the first preachers of the Christian religion in the early days of the Church.

"I was incredulous at first," continued the priest, "until I saw these things for myself. An old father of our mission rebuked me for it. 'You are an ignorant fellow,' he said, 'your airs are still of the seminary.' And what he said was just, my friends.

"On one Monday morning as we met for our council, I could see that this old priest had something to say. M. Lasserre was his name. He kept very silent until the little businesses had been accomplished, and then he turned to the Father Rector.

"'Monseigneur has written,' he said, 'and given me the necessary permission for the matter you know, my father. And he bids me take another priest with me. I ask that Father Meuron may accompany me. He needs a lesson, this zealous young missionary.'

"The Father Rector smiled at me, as I sat astonished, and nodded at Father Lasserre to give permission.

"'Father Lasserre will explain all to you,' he said, as he stood up for the prayer.

"The good priest explained all to me as the Father Rector had directed.

"It appeared that there was a matter of exorcism on hand. A woman who lived with her mother and husband had been afflicted by the devil, Father Lasserre said. She was a catechumen, and had been devout for several months and all seemed well, until this—this assault had been made on her soul. Father Lasserre had visited the woman and examined her, and had made his report to the bishop, asking permission to exorcise the creature, and it was this permission that had been sent on that morning.

"I did not venture to tell the priest that he was mistaken and that the affair was one of epilepsy. I had studied a little in books for my medical training, and all that I heard now seemed to confirm me in the diagnosis. There were the symptoms, easy to read. What would you have?"—the priest again made his little gesture—"I knew more in my youth than all the Fathers of the Church. Their affairs of devils were nothing but an affection of the brain, dreams and fancies! And if the exorcisms had appeared to be of direct service to such folk, it was from the effect of the solemnity upon the mind. It was no more."

He laughed with a fierce irony.

"You know it all, gentlemen!"

I had lost all desire to sleep now. The French priest was more interesting than I had thought. His elaborateness seemed dissipated; his voice trembled a little as he arraigned his own conceit, and I began to wonder how this change of mind had been wrought.

"We set out that afternoon," he continued. "The woman lived on the farther side of the island, perhaps a couple of hours' travel, for it was rough going; and as we went up over the path, Father Lasserre told me more.

"It seemed that the woman blasphemed. (The subconscious self, said I to myself, as M. Charcot has explained. It is her old habit reasserting itself.)

"She foamed and rolled her eyes. (An affection of the brain, said I.)

"She feared holy water: they dared not throw it on her, her struggles were so fierce. (Because she has been taught to fear it, said I.)

"And so the good father talked, eyeing me now and again; and I smiled in my heart, knowing that he was a simple old fellow who had not studied the new books.

"She was quieter after sunset, he told me, and would take a little food then. Her fits came on her for the most part at midday. And I smiled again at that. Why it should be so, I knew. The heat affected her. She would be quieter, science would tell us, when evening fell. If it were the power of Satan that held her, she would surely rage more in the darkness than in the light. The Scriptures tell us so.

"I said something of this to Father Lasserre, as if it were a question, and he looked at me.

"'Perhaps, brother,' he said, 'she is more at ease in the darkness and fears the light, and that she is quieter therefore when the sun sets.'

"Again I smiled to myself. What piety, said I, and what foolishness!

"The house where the three lived stood apart from any others. It was an old shed into which they had moved a week before, for the neighbours could no longer bear the woman's screaming. And we came to it toward sunset.

"It was a heavy evening, dull and thick, and as we pushed down the path I saw the smoking mountain high on the left hand between the tangled trees. There was a great silence round us, and no wind, and every leaf against the angry sky was as if cut of steel.

"We saw the roof below us presently, and a little smoke escaped from a hole, for there was no chimney.

"'We will sit here a little, brother,' said my friend. 'We will not enter till sunset.'

"And he took out his Office book and began to say his Matins and Lauds, sitting on a fallen tree trunk by the side of the path.

"All was very silent about us. I suffered terrible distractions, for I was a young man and excited; and though I knew it was no more than epilepsy that I was to see, yet epilepsy is not a good sight to regard. But I was finishing the first nocturn when I saw that Father Lasserre was looking off his book.

"We were sitting thirty yards from the roof of the hut which was built in a scoop of the ground, so that the roof was level with the ground on which we sat. Below it was a little open space, flat, perhaps twenty yards across, and below that yet farther was the wood again, and far over that was the smoke of the village against the sea. There was the mouth of a well with a bucket beside it; and by this was standing a man, a negro, very upright, with a vessel in his hand.

"This fellow turned as I looked, and saw us there, and he dropped the vessel, and I could see his white teeth. Father Lasserre stood up and laid his finger on his lips, nodded once or twice, pointed to the west where the sun was just above the horizon, and the fellow nodded to us again and stooped for his vessel.

"He filled it from the bucket and went back into the house.

"I looked at Father Lasserre, and he looked at me.

"'In five minutes,' he said. 'That is the husband. Did you not see his wounds?'

"I had seen no more than his teeth, I said, and my friend nodded again and proceeded to finish his nocturn."

Again Father Meuron paused dramatically. His ruddy face seemed a little pale in the candle-light, although he had told us nothing yet that could account for his apparent horror. Plainly something was coming soon.

The Rector leaned back to me and whispered behind his hand in reference to what the Frenchman had related a few minutes before, that no priest was allowed to use exorcism without the special leave of the bishop. I nodded and thanked him.

Father Meuron flashed his eyes dreadfully round the circle, clasped his hands and continued:

"When the sun showed only a red rim above the sea we went down to the house. The path ran on high ground to the roof, and then dipped down the edge of the cutting past the window to the front of the shed.

"I looked through this window sideways as I went after Father Lasserre who was carrying his bag with the book and the holy water, but I could see nothing but the light of the fire. And there was no sound. That was terrible to me!

"The door was closed as we came to it, and as Father Lasserre lifted his hand to knock there was the howl of a beast from within.

"He knocked and looked at me.

"'It is but epilepsy,' he said, and his lips wrinkled as he said it."

The priest stopped again, and smiled ironically at us all. Then he clasped his hands beneath his chin, like a man in terror.

"I will not tell you all that I saw," he went on, "when the candle was lighted and set on the table; but only a little. You would not dream well, my friends—as I did not that night.

"But the woman sat in a corner by the fireplace, bound with cords by her arms to the back of the chair, and her feet to the legs of it.

"Gentlemen, she was like no woman at all. The howl of a wolf came from her lips, but there were words in the howl. At first I could not understand, till she began in French—and then I understood—my God!

"The foam dripped from her mouth like water, and her eyes—but there! I began to shake when I saw them until the holy water was spilled on the floor, and I set it down on the table by the candle. There was a plate of meat on the table, roasted mutton, I think, and a loaf of bread beside it. Remember that, gentlemen! That mutton and bread! And as I stood there, I told myself, like making acts of faith, that it was but epilepsy, or at the most madness.

"My friends, it is probable that few of you know the form of exorcism. It is neither in the Ritual nor the Pontifical, and I cannot remember it all myself. But it began thus."

The Frenchman sprang up and stood with his back to the fire, with his face in shadow.

"Father Lasserre was here where I stand, in his cotta

and stole, and I beside him. There where my chair stands was the square table, as near as that, with the bread and meat and the holy water and the candle. Beyond the table was the woman; her husband stood beside her on the left hand, and the old mother was there"—he flung out a hand to the right—"on the floor, telling her beads and weeping—but weeping!

"When the Father was ready and had said a word to the others, he signed to me to lift the holy water again—she was quiet at the moment—and then he sprinkled her.

"As he lifted his hand she raised her eyes, and there was a look in them of terror, as if at a blow, and as the drops fell she leapt forward in the chair, and the chair leapt with her. Her husband was at her and dragged the chair back. But, my God! It was terrible to see him, his teeth shone as if he smiled, but the tears ran down his face.

"Then she moaned like a child in pain. It was as if the holy water burned her; she lifted her face to her man as if she begged him to wipe off the drops.

"And all the while I still told myself that it was the terror of her mind only at the holy water—that it could not be that she was possessed by Satan—it was but madness—madness and epilepsy!

"Father Lasserre went on with the prayers, and I said *Amen,* and there was a psalm—*in nomine tuo salvum me fac*—and then came the first bidding to the unclean spirit to go out, in the name of the Mysteries of the Incarnation and Passion.

"Gentlemen, I swear to you that something happened then, but I do not know what. A confusion fell on me and a kind of darkness. I saw nothing—it was as if I were dead."

The priest lifted a shaking hand to wipe off the sweat from his forehead. There was a profound silence in the room. I looked once at Monsignor and he was holding his pipe an inch off his mouth, and his lips were slack and open as he stared.

"Then when I knew where I was, Father Lasserre was reading out of the Gospels; how our Lord gave authority to His Church to cast out unclean spirits; and all the while his voice never trembled."

"And the woman?" said a voice hoarsely from Father Brent's chair.

"Ah, the woman! My God! I do not know. I did not look at her. I stared at the plate on the table; but at least she was not crying out now.

"When the Scripture was finished, Father Lasserre gave me the book.

"'Bah, Father!' he said. 'It is but epilepsy, is it not?'

"Then he beckoned me, and I went with him holding the book till we were within a yard of the woman. But I could not hold the book still, it shook, it shook—"

Father Meuron thrust out his hand—"It shook like that, gentlemen.

"He took the book from me, sharply and angrily. 'Go back, sir,' he said, and he thrust the book into the husband's hand.

"'There,' he said.

"I went back behind the table and leaned on it.

"Then Father Lasserre—my God, the courage of this man!—he set his hands on the woman's head. She writhed up her teeth to bite, but he was too strong for her, and then he cried out from the book the second bidding to the unclean spirit.

"'*Ecce crucem Domini!* Behold the Cross of the Lord! Flee, ye adverse hosts! The lion of the tribe of Judah hath prevailed!'

"Gentlemen"—the Frenchman flung out his hands— "I who stand here tell you that something happened—God knows what—I only know this, that as the woman cried out and scrambled with her feet on the floor, the flame of the candle became smoke-coloured for one instant. I told myself it was the dust of her struggling and her foul breath. Yes, gentlemen, as you tell yourselves now. Bah! It is but epilepsy, is it not so, sir?"

The old Rector leaned forward with a deprecating hand, but the Frenchman glared and gesticulated; there was a murmur from the room, and the old priest leaned back again and propped his head on his band.

"Then there was a prayer. I heard *Oremus,* but I did not dare to look at the woman. I fixed my eyes so, on the bread and meat: it was the one clean thing in that terrible room. I whispered to myself, 'Bread and mutton, bread and mutton.' I thought of the refectory at home—anything— you understand me, gentlemen, anything familiar to quiet myself.

"Then there was the third exorcism."

I saw the Frenchman's hands rise and fall, clenched, and his teeth close on his lip to stay its trembling. He swallowed in his throat once or twice.

"Gentlemen, I swear to you by God Almighty that this was what I saw. I kept my eyes on the bread and meat. It lay there, beneath my eyes, and yet I saw too the good Father Lasserre lean forward to the woman again, and heard him begin, '*Exorcizo te...*'

"And then this happened—this happened..."

"The bread and the meat corrupted themselves to worms before my eyes...."

Father Meuron dashed forward, turned round, and dropped into his chair as the two English priests on either side sprang to their feet.

In a few minutes he was able to tell us that all had ended well; that the woman had been presently found in her right mind, after an incident or two that I will take leave to omit; and that the apparent paroxysm of nature that had accompanied the words of the third exorcism had passed away as suddenly as it had come.

Then we went to night prayers and fortified ourselves against the dark.

III

Father Brent's Tale

IT was universally voted on Monday that the Englishman should follow Father Meuron, and we looked with some satisfaction on his wholesome face and steady blue eyes, as he took up his tale after supper.

"Mine is a very poor story," he began, "after the one we heard on Saturday, and, what is worse, there is no explanation that I have ever heard that seemed to me adequate. Perhaps someone will supply one this evening. I feel very much like the ant in London whom Monsignor has such sympathy with."

He drew at his cigarette, smiling, and we settled ourselves down with looks of resolute science on our features. I at least was conscious of wishing to wear one.

"After my ordination to the subdiaconate I was in England for the summer and went down to stay with a friend on the Fal, at the beginning of October.

"My friend's house stood on a spot of land running out into the estuary; there was a beech-wood behind it and on either side. There was a small embankment on which the building actually stood, of which the sea-wall ran straight down on to the rocks, so that at high tide the water came halfway up the stonework. There was a large smoking room looking the same way, and a little paved path separated its windows from the low wall. We had a series of very warm days when I was there, and after dinner we would sit outside in the dark and listen to the water lapping below. There was another house on the further side of the river, about half a mile away, and we could see its lights sometimes. About three miles up stream—that is, on our right—lay Truro, and Falmouth, as far as I remember, about four miles to the left. But we were entirely cut off from our neighbours by the beech-woods all round us, and, except for the house opposite, might have been clean out of civilization."

Father Brent tossed away his cigarette and lit another.

He seemed a very sensible person, I thought, unlike the excitable Frenchman, and his manner of speaking was serene and practical.

"My friend was a widower," he went on, "but had one boy, about eleven years old, who, I remember, was to go to school after Christmas. I asked Franklyn, my friend, why Jack had not gone before, and he told me, as parents will, that he was a peculiarly sensitive boy, a little hysterical at times and very nervous, but he was less so than he used to be and probably, his father said, if he was allowed time, school would be the best thing for him. Up to the present, however, he had shrunk from sending him.

"'He has extraordinary fancies,' he said, 'and thinks he sees things. The other day—' and then Jack came in, and he stopped, and I clean forgot to ask him afterwards what he was going to say.

"Now if anyone here has ever been to Cornwall, he will know what a queer county it is. It is cram-full of legends and so on. Every one who has ever been there seems to have left his mark. You get the Phoenicians in goodness knows what century; they came there for tin, and some of the mines still in work are supposed to have been opened by them. Cornish cream too seems to have been brought there by them—for I need not tell you perhaps that the stuff is originally Cornish and not Devon. Then Solomon, some think, sent ships there—though personally I believe that is nonsense; but you get some curious names—Marazion, for instance, which means the bitterness of Zion. That has made some believe that the Cornish are the lost tribes. Then you get a connexion with both Ireland and Brittany in names, language, and beliefs, and so on—I could go on forever. They still talk of 'going to England' when they cross the border into Devonshire.

"Then the people are very odd—real Celts—with a genius for religion and the supernatural generally. They believe in pixies; they have got a hundred saints and holy wells and holy trees that no one else has ever heard of. They have the most astonishing old churches. There is one convent—at Lanherne I think—where the Blessed Sacrament has remained with its light burning right up to the present. And lastly, all the people are furious Wesleyans.

"So the whole place is a confusion of history, a sort of palimpsest, as the Father Rector here would tell us. A cross you find in the moor may be pagan, or Catholic, or Anglican, or most likely all three together. And that is what makes an explanation of what I am going to tell you such a difficult thing.

"I did not know much about this when I went there on the third of October, but Franklyn told me a lot, and he took me about to one or two places—here and there—to Truro to see the new Cathedral, to Perranzabuloe where there is an old mystery theatre and a church in the sands, and so on. And one day we rowed down to Falmouth.

"The estuary is a lovely place when the tide is in. You find the odd combination of seaweed and beech trees growing almost together. The trees stand with their roots in saltish water, and the creeks run right up into the woods. But it is terrible when the tide is out—great sheets of mud, with wreckage sticking up, and draggled weed, and mussels, and so on.

"About the end of my first week it was high tide after dinner, and we sat out on the terrace looking across the water. We could hear it lapping below, and the moon was just coming up behind the house. I tossed over my cigarette end and heard it fizz in the water, and then I put out my hand to the box for another. There wasn't one, and Franklyn said he would go indoors to find some. He thought he had some Nestors in his bedroom.

"So Franklyn went in and I was left alone. It was perfectly quiet: there was not a ripple on the water, which was about eight feet below me, as I got up from my chair and sat on the low wall. There was a sort of glimmer on the water from the moon behind, and I could see a yellow streak clean across the surface from the house opposite among the black woods. It was as warm as summer too."

Father Brent threw his cigarette away, and sat a little forward in his chair. I began to feel more interested. He was plainly interested himself, for he clasped his hands round a knee, and gave a quick look into our faces. Then he looked back again at the fire as he went on.

"Then across the streak of yellow fight and where the moon glimmered, I saw a kind of black line, moving. It was coming toward me, and there seemed to be a sort of disturbance behind. I stood up and waited, wondering what it was. I could hear Franklyn pulling out a drawer in the bedroom overhead, but everything else was deadly still.

"As I stood, it came nearer swiftly; it was just a high ripple in the water, and a moment later the flat surface below heaved up, and I could hear it lapping and splashing on the face of the wall.

"It was exactly as if some big ship had gone up the estuary. I strained my eyes out, but there was nothing to be seen. There was the glimmer of the moon on the water, the houselights burning half a mile away, and the black woods beyond. There was a beach, rocks, and shingle on my right, curving along toward a place called Meopas; and I could hear the wave hiss and clatter all along it as it went upstream.

"Then I sat down again.

"I cannot say I was exactly frightened; but I was very much puzzled. It surely could not be a tidal wave; there was certainly no ship; it could not be anything swimming, for the wave was like the wave of a really large vessel.

"In a minute or two Franklyn came down with the Nestors, and I told him. He laughed at me. He said it must have been a breeze, or the turn of the tide, or something. Then he said he had been in to look at Jack, and had found him in a sort of nightmare, tossing and moaning; he had not wakened him, he said, but just touched him and said a word or two, and the boy had turned over and gone to sleep.

"But I would not let him change the subject. I persisted it had been a really big wash of some kind.

"He stared at me.

"'Take a cigarette,' he said, 'I found them at last under a hat.'

"But I went on at him. It had made an impression on me, and I was a little uncomfortable.

"'It is bosh,' he said. 'But we will go and see if you like. The wall will be wet if there was a big wave.'

"He fetched a lantern, and we went down the steps that led round the side of the embankment into the water. I went first, until my feet were on the last step above the water. He carried the lantern.

"Then I heard him exclaim:

"'You are standing in a pool,' he said.

"I looked down and saw that it was so; the steps, three of them at least, were shining in the light of the lantern.

"I put out my hand for the lantern, held on to a ring by my left hand, and leaned out as far as I could, looking at the face of the wall. It was wet and dripping for at least four feet above the mark of the high tide.

"I told him, and he came down and looked too, and then we went up again to the house.

"We neither of us said very much more that evening. The only suggestion that Franklyn could make was that it must have been a very odd kind of tidal wave. For myself, I knew nothing about tidal waves; but I gathered from his tone that this certainly could not have been one.

"We sat out about half an hour more, but there was no sound again.

"When we went up to bed we peeped into Jack's room. He was lying perfectly quiet on his right side, turned away from the window which was open, but there was a little frown, I thought, on his forehead, and his eyes seemed screwed up."

The priest stopped again.

We were all very quiet. The story was not exciting, but it was distinctly interesting, and I could see the others were puzzled. Perhaps what impressed us most was the very matter-of-fact tone in which the story was told.

The Rector put in a word during the silence.

"How do you know it was not a tidal wave?" he asked.

"It may have been, Father," said the young priest. "But that is not the end."

He filled his lungs with smoke, blew it out, and went on.

Nothing whatever of any interest happened for the next day or two, except that Franklyn asked a boatman at Meopas whether he had heard anything of a wave on the Monday night. The man looked at us and shook his head, still looking at us oddly.

"'I was in bed early,' he said.

"On the Thursday afternoon Franklyn got a note asking him to dine in Truro, to meet someone who had come down from town. I told him to go, of course, and he went off in his dog-cart about half-past six.

"Jack and I dined together at half-past seven, and, I may say, we made friends. He was less shy when his father was away. I think Franklyn laughed at him a little too much, hoping to cure him of his fancies.

"The boy told me some of them, though, that night. I don't remember any of them particularly, but I do remember the general effect, and I was really impressed by the sort of insight he seemed to have into things. He said some curious things about trees and their characters. Perhaps you remember MacDonald's *Phantasies*. It was rather like that. He was fond of beeches, I gathered, and thought himself safe in them; he liked to climb them and to think that the house was surrounded by them. And there was a lot of things like that he said. I remember too that he hated cypresses and cats and the twilight.

"'But I am not afraid of the dark,' he said. 'I like the dark as much as the light, and I always sleep with my windows open and no curtains.'"

Monsignor Maxwell nodded abruptly. I could see he was watching.

"I know," he said. "I knew another child like that."

"Well," went on Father Brent, "the boy said good night and went to bed about nine. I sat in the smoking room a bit, for it had turned a little cold, and about ten stepped out onto the terrace.

"It was perfectly still and cloudy. I forget whether there was a moon. At any rate I did not see it. There was just the black gulf of water, with the line of light across it from the house opposite. Then I went indoors and shut the windows.

"I read again for a while, and finished my book. I had

said my Office, so I looked about for another novel. Then I remembered there had been one I wanted to read in Franklyn's room overhead, so I took a candle and went up. Jack's room was over the smoking room, and his father's was beyond it on the right, and there was a door between them. Both faced the front, remember.

"Franklyn's room had three windows, two looking on to the river and one upstream toward Truro, over the beach I spoke of before. I went in there; and saw that the door was open between the two rooms, so I slipped off my shoes for fear of disturbing the boy, and went across to the bookshelf that stood between the two front windows. All three windows were open. Franklyn was mad about fresh air.

"I was bending down to look at the backs of the books, and had my finger on the one I wanted when I heard a kind of moan from the boy's room.

"I stood up, startled, and it came again. Why, he had had a nightmare only three days before, I remembered. As I stood there wondering whether it would be kind to wake him, I heard another sound.

"It was a noise that came through the side window that looked up the beach, and it was the noise of a breaking wave."

The priest made a momentary pause, and, as he flicked the end of his cigarette, I saw his fingers tremble very slightly.

"I didn't hesitate then, but went straight into the room next door, and as I went across the floor heard the boy moaning and tossing. It was pitch dark and I could see nothing. I was thinking that tidal waves don't come downstream.

"Then my knees struck the edge of the bed.

"'Jack,' I said, 'Jack.'

"There was a rustle from the bed-clothes, and (I should have thought) long before he could have awakened, I heard his feet on the floor, and then felt him brush past me. Then I saw him outlined against the pale window with his hands on the glass over his head. Then I was by him, taking care not to touch him.

"All this took about five seconds, I suppose, from the time when I heard the wave on the beach. I stared out now over the boy's head, but there was nothing in the world to be seen but the black water and the glimmer of the light across it.

"Jack was perfectly silent, but I could see that he was watching. He didn't seem to know I was there.

"Then I whispered to him rather sharply.

"'What is it, Jack? What do you see?'

"He said nothing, and I repeated my question.

"Then he answered, almost as if talking to himself: 'Ships,' he said, 'three ships.'

"Now I swear there was nothing there. I thought it was a nightmare.

"'Nonsense,' I said. 'How can you see them? It's too dark.'

"'A light in each,' he said, 'in the bows—blazing!'

"As he said it I saw his head turning slowly to the left as if he was following them. Then there came the sound of the wave breaking on the stonework just below the windows.

"'Are you frightened?' I said suddenly.

"'Yes,' said the boy.

"'Why?'

"'I don't know.'

"Then I saw his hands come down from the window and cover his face, and he began to moan again.

"'Come back to bed,' I said, but I daren't touch him. I could see he was sleep-walking.

"Then he turned, went straight across the room, still making an odd sound, and I heard him climb into bed.

"I covered him up, and went out."

Father Brent stopped again. He had rather a curious look in his face, and I saw that his cigarette had gone out. None of us spoke or moved.

Then he went on again, abruptly:

"Well, you know, I didn't know I was frightened exactly until I came out onto the landing. There was a tall glass there on the right hand of the staircase, and just as I came opposite I thought I heard the hiss of the wave again, and I nearly screamed. It was only the wheels of Franklyn's dog-cart coming up the drive, but as I looked in the glass I saw that my face was like paper. We had a long talk about the Phoenicians that evening. Franklyn looked them out in the Encyclopaedia, but there was nothing particularly interesting."

"Well, that's all. Give me a match, Father. This beastly thing's gone out. It's a *spaghetto*."

We had no theories to suggest. Monsignor was temerarious enough to remark that the story was an excellent illustration of his own views.

IV

The Father Rector's Story

The Father Rector of San Filippo was an old man, a Canadian by birth, who had been educated in England, but he had worked in many parts of the world since receiving the priesthood nearly fifty years ago, and for my part I certainly expected that he would have many experiences to relate.

At first, however, he entirely refused to tell a story. He said he had had an uneventful life, that he could not compete with the tales he had heard. But persuasion proved too strong, and on going in to see him on another matter one morning I found him at his tin dispatch-box with a diary in his hand.

"I have found something that I think may do," he said, "if no one else has promised for this evening. It is really the only thing approaching the preternatural I have ever experienced."

I congratulated him and ourselves; and the same evening after supper he told his story, with the diary beside him to which he referred now and then. (I shall omit his irrelevancies, of which there were a good many.)

"This happened to me," he said, "nearly thirty years ago. I had been twenty years a priest, and was working in a town mission in the south of England. I made the acquaintance of a Catholic family who had a large country house about ten miles away. They were not very fervent people, but they had a chapel in the house where I would say Mass sometimes on Sundays, when I could get away from my own church on Saturday night.

"On one of these occasions I met for the first time an artist, whose name you would all know if I mentioned it, but it will be convenient to call him Mr. Farquharson. He made an extremely unpleasant impression on me, and yet there was no reason for it that I could see. He was a big man, palish, with curling brown hair. He was always very well-dressed, with a suspicion of scent about him; he talked extremely wittily and would say the most surprising things that were at once brilliant and dangerous; and yet in his talk he never transgressed good manners. In fact he was very cordial always to me; he seemed to go out of his way to be courteous and friendly, and yet I could not bear the fellow. However. I tried to conceal that, and with some success, as you will see.

"I was astonished that he asked me no questions about our beliefs or practices. Such people generally do, you know, and they profess to admire our worship and its dignity. In the evening he played and sang magnificently; very touching and pathetic songs, as a rule.

"On the following morning he attended Mass, but I did not think much of that. Guests generally do, I have found, in Catholic houses. Then I went off in the afternoon back to my mission.

"I suppose it was six weeks before I met him again, and then it was at the same place. My hostess gave me tea alone, for I arrived late; and as we sat in the hall she told me that Mr. Farquharson was there again. Then she added to my surprise that he had expressed a great liking for me, and had come down from town partly with the hope of meeting me. She went on talking about him for a while; told me that three of his pictures had been taken again by the French Salon, and at last told me that he had been baptized and educated as a Catholic, but had for many years ceased to practise his religion. She had only learnt this recently.

"Well, that explained a good deal; and I was greatly taken aback. I did not quite know how to act. But she talked on about him a little, and I became sorry for the man and determined that I would make no difference in my behaviour toward him. From what she said, I gathered that it might be in my power to win him back. He had everything against him, she told me."

"Now let me tell you a word about his pictures. I had seen them here and there, as well as reproductions of them, as all the world had at that time, and they were very remarkable. They were on extraordinarily simple and innocent subjects—and often religious—a child going to First Communion; a knight riding on a lonely road; a boy warming his hands at the fire; a woman praying. There was not a line or a colour in them that anyone could dislike, and yet—yet they were corrupt. I know nothing about art; but it needed no art to see that these were corrupt. I did not understand it then, and I do not now; but—well, there it is. I cannot describe their effect on me; but I know that many others felt the same, and I believe that kind of painting is not uncommon in the French School."

The priest paused a moment.

"As I went down the long passage to the smoking room, I declare that I was not thinking of this side of the man. I was only wondering whether I could do anything, but the moment I came in, and found him standing alone on the hearthrug, all this leapt back into my mind.

"His personality was exactly like his own pictures. There was nothing that one could point to in his face and say that it revealed his character. It did not. It was a clean-shaven, clever face, strong and artistic; his hand, as he took mine, was firm and slender and strong too. And yet—yet my flesh crept at him. It seemed to me he was a kind of devil.

"Again I did my utmost to hide all this, as we sat and talked that evening till the dressing-gong rang, and again I succeeded, but it was a sore effort. Once when he put his hand on my arm I nearly jerked it off, so great was the horror it gave me.

"I did not sit near him at dinner; there were several people dining there that night, but our host was unwell and went to bed early, and this man and myself, after he had played and sung an hour or so in the drawing room, talked till late in the smoking room and all the while the horror grew; I have never felt anything like it.

I am generally fairly placid; but it was all I could do to keep quiet. I even wondered once or twice whether it was not my duty to tell him plainly what I felt, to—to—well, really this sounds absurd—but to curse him as an unclean

and corrupt creature who had lost faith and grace and
everything, and was on the very brink of eternal fire."

The old man's voice rang with emotion. I had never seen
him so much moved, and was astonished at his vehemence.

"Well, thank God! I did not!

"At last it came out that I knew about his having been
a Catholic. I did not tell him where I had learnt it, but per-
haps he suspected. Of course, though, I might have learnt
it in a hundred ways.

"He seemed very much surprised—not at my knowing,
but at my treating him as I did. It seemed that he had met
with unpleasantness more than once at the hands of priests
who knew.

"Well, to cut it short, before I went away next day he
asked me to call upon him sometime at his house in Lon-
don, and he asked me in such a way that I knew he meant
it."

The priest stopped and referred to his diary. Then he
went on.

"It was in the following May, six months later, that I
fulfilled my promise.

"It may have been association, and what I suspected of
the man, but the house almost terrified me by its beauty
and its simplicity and its air of corruption. And yet there
was nothing to account for it. There was not a picture in
it, as far as I could see, that had anything in it to which
even a priest could object. There was a long gallery leading
from the front door, floored, ceiled, and walled with oak
in little panels, with pictures in each along the two sides,

chiefly, I should suppose now, of that same French School of which I have spoken. There was an exquisite crucifix at the end, and yet, in some strange way, even that seemed to be tainted. I felt I suppose in the manner that Father Stein described to us when he mentioned Benares; and yet there, I have heard, the pictures and carvings correspond with the sensation, and here they did not.

"He received me in his studio at the end of the passage. There was a great painting on an easel, on which he was working, a painting of Our Lady going to the well at Nazareth—most exquisite, and yet terrible. I could hardly keep my eyes off it. It was nearly finished, he told me. And there was his grand piano against the wall.

"Well, we sat and talked, and before I left that evening I knew everything. He did not tell me in confession, and the story became notorious after his death a few months later; but yet I can tell you no more now than that all I had felt about him was justified by what I heard. Part of what the world did not hear would not have seemed important to any but a priest; it was just the history of his own soul, apart from his deeds, the history of his wanton contempt of light and warnings. And I heard more besides too, that I cannot bear to think of even now."

The priest stopped again; and I could see his lips were trembling with emotion. We were all very quiet ourselves; the effect on my mind at least was extraordinary. Presently he went on:

"Before I left I persuaded him to go to confession. The man had not really lost faith for a moment, so far as I could gather. I learnt, from details that I cannot even hint at, that he had known it all to be true, pitilessly clearly, in his worst moments. Grace had been prevailing, especially of late, and he was sick of his life. Of course he had tried to stifle conscience, but by the mercy of God he had failed. I cannot imagine why, except that there is no end to the loving kindness of God, but I have known many souls not half so evil as his, lose their faith and their whole spiritual sense beyond all human hope of recovery."

The priest stopped again; turned over several pages of his diary, and as he did so I saw him stop once or twice and read silently to himself, his lips moving.

"I must miss out a great deal here. He did not come to confession to me, but to a Carthusian, after a retreat. I need not go into all the details of that so far as I knew them, and I will skip another six months.

"During that time I wrote to him more than once, and just got a line or two back. Then I was ordered abroad, and when we touched at Brindisi I received a letter from him."

The priest lifted his diary again near his eyes. "Here is one sentence," he said. "Listen: 'I know I am forgiven; but the punishment is driving me mad. What would you say if you knew all! I cannot write it. I wonder if we shall meet again. I wonder what you would say.'

"There was more that I cannot read; but it offers no explanation of this sentence. I wrote of course at once, and said I would be home in four months, and asked for an explanation. I did not hear again, though I wrote three or four times; and after three or four months in Malta I went back to England.

"My first visit was to Mr. Farquharson, when I had

written to prepare him for my coming."

The old man stopped again, and I could see he was finding it more and more difficult to speak. He looked at the diary again once or twice, but I could see that it was only to give himself time to recover. Then he lowered it once more, leaned his elbow on the chair arm, and his head on his hand, and went on in a slow voice full of effort:

"The first change was in the gallery; his pictures were all gone, and in their place hung others—engravings and portraits of no interest or beauty that I could see. The crucifix was gone, and in its place stood another very simple and common—a plaster figure on a black cross. It was all very commonplace—such a room as you might see in any house. The man took me through as before, but instead of opening the studio door, as I expected, turned up the stairs on the right, and I followed. He stopped at a little door at the end of a short passage, tapped, and threw it open. He announced my name and I went in."

He paused once more.

"There was a Japanese screen in front of me and I went round it, wondering what I should find. I caught a sight of a simple commonplace room with a window looking out on my left, and then I saw an old man sitting in a high chair over the fire on which boiled a saucepan, warming his hands, with a rug over his knees. His face was turned to me, but it was that of a stranger.

"There was a table between us, and I stood hesitating, on the point of apologizing, and the old man looked at me smiling.

"'You do not know me,' he said.

"Then I saw it bore an odd sort of resemblance to Mr. Farquharson; and I supposed it was his father. That would account for the mistake too, I thought in a moment. My letter must have been delivered to him instead.

"'I came to see Mr. Farquharson,' I said. 'I beg your pardon if—'

"Then he interrupted me—well, you will guess—this was the man I had come to see. It took a minute or two before I could realize it. I swear to you that the man looked, not ten, nor twenty, nor thirty, but fifty years older.

"I went and took his hand and sat down, but I could not say a word. Then he told me his story, and as he told it I watched him. I looked at his face; it had been full and generous in its lines, now the skin was drawn tightly over his cheeks and great square jaw. His hair, so much of it as escaped under his stuff cap, was snow-white and like silk. His hands, stretched over the fire, were gnarled and veined and tremulous. And all this had come to him in less than one year.

"Well, this was his story. His health had failed abruptly within a month of my last sight of him. He had noticed weakness coming on soon after his reconciliation, and the failure of his powers had increased like lightning.

"I will tell you what first flashed into my mind, that it was merely a sudden unprecedented breakdown that had first given room for grace to reassert itself, and had then normally gone forward. The life he had led—well, you understand.

"Then he told me a few more facts that soon put that thought out of my head. All his artistic powers had gone too. He gave me an example.

"'Look round this room,' he said in his old man's voice, 'and tell me frankly what you think of it—the pictures— the furniture.'

"I did so, and was astonished at their ugliness. There were a couple of hideous oleographs on the wall opposite the window—perhaps you know them—of the tombs of Our Lord and His Blessed Mother, with yellow candle- sticks standing upon them. There were green baize curtains by the windows; an Axminster carpet of vivid colours on the floor; a mahogany table in the centre with a breviary upon it and a portfolio open. It was the kind of a room that you might find in twenty houses in a row on the outskirts of a colliery town.

"I supposed of course that he had furnished his room like this out of a morbid kind of mortification, and I hinted this to him.

"He smiled again, but he looked puzzled.

"'No,' he said, 'indeed not. Then you do think them ugly too? Well, well. It is that I do not care. Will you believe me when I tell you that? There is no asceticism in the matter. Those pictures seem to me as good as any oth- ers. I have sold the others.'

"'But you know they are not good,' I said.

"'My friends tell me so, and I remember I used to think so once too. But that has all gone. Besides, I like them.'

"He turned in his chair and opened the portfolio that lay by him.

"'Look,' he said, and pushed it over to me, watching my face as I took it.

"It was full of sheets of paper, scrawled with such pictures as a stupid child might draw. There was not the faintest trace of any power in them. Here is one of them that he gave me." (He drew out a paper from his diary and held it up.) "I will show it you presently.

"As I looked at them it suddenly struck me that all this was an elaborate pose. I suppose I showed the thought in the way I glanced up at him. At any rate he knew it. He smiled again, pitifully.

"'No,' he said, 'it is not a pose. I have posed for forty years, but I have forgotten how to do it now. It does not seem to me worth while, either.'

"'Are you happy?' I asked.

"'Oh! I suppose so,' he said.

"I sat there bewildered.

"'And music?' I said.

"He made a little gesture with his old hands.

"'Tell Jackson to let you see the piano in the studio,' he said, 'as you go downstairs. And you might look at the picture of Our Lady at Nazareth at the same time. You will see how I tried to go on with it. My friends tell me it is all wrong, and asked me to stop. I supposed they knew, so I stopped.'

"Well, we talked a while and I learnt how all was with him. He believed with his whole being, and that was all. He received the Sacraments once a week, and he was happy in a subdued kind of way. There was no ecstasy of happiness; there was no torment from the imagination, such as is usual in these cases of conversion. He had suffered agonies at first from the loss of his powers, as he realized that his natural perceptions were gone, and it was then that he had written to me."

The Rector stopped again a moment, fingering the paper.

"I saw his doctor, of course, and—"

Monsignor broke in. I noticed that he had been listening intently.

"The piano and the picture?" he said.

"Ah, yes! Well, the piano was just a box of strings; many of the notes were broken and the other wires were hopelessly out of tune. They were broken, the man told me, within a week or two of his master's change of life—he spoke quite frankly to me—Mr. Farquharson had tried to play, it seemed, and could scarcely play a right note, and in a passion of anger, it was supposed, had smashed the notes with his fists. And the picture—well, it was a miserable sight—there was a tawdry sort of crown, ill-drawn and ill-coloured on her head, and a terrible sort of cherub painted all across the sky. Someone else, it seemed, had tried to paint these out, which increased the confusion.

"The doctor told me it was softening of the brain. I asked him honestly to tell me whether he had ever come across such a case before, and he confessed he had not.

"It took me a week or two, and another conversation with Mr. Farquharson before I understood what it all meant. It was not natural, the doctor assured me, and it could scarcely be that Almighty God had arbitrarily inflicted such a punishment. And then I thought I understood—as no doubt you have all done before this."

The old priest's voice had an air of finality in his last

sentence, and he handed the scrap of paper to Father Bianchi, who sat beside him.

"One moment, Father," I said, "I do not understand at all."

The priest turned to me, and his eyes were full of tears.

"Why this is my reading of it," he said. "This man had been one mass of corruption, body, mind and soul. Every power of his had been nurtured on evil for thirty years. Then he made his effort and the evil was withdrawn—and—and, well he fell to pieces. The only thing that was alive in him was the life of grace. There was nothing else to live. He died, too, three months later, tolerably happy, I think."

As I pondered this the paper was handed to me, and I looked at it in bewildered silence. It was a head, grotesque in its feebleness and lack of art. There was a crown of thorns about it, and an inscription in a child's handwriting below: *Deus in virtute Tua salvum me fac!*

Then my own eyes were full of tears too.

V

Father Girdlestone's Tale

I

"I have found another *raconteur* for this evening," said Monsignor as he came in to dinner on the following day, "but he cannot be here till late."

The Rector looked up questioningly.

"Yes, I know," said Monsignor unfolding his napkin. "But it is a long story; it will take at least two nights; but—but it is a beauty, reverend Fathers."

We murmured appreciatively.

"I heard him tell it twenty years ago," proceeded the priest, "I was a boy then....I had a bad night after it, I remember. But the first part is rather dull."

The appreciative murmur was even louder.

"Well, then. Is that settled?"

We assented.

The entrance of Father Girdlestone that evening was somewhat dramatic. We were all talking briskly together in our wide semicircle, when Father Brent uttered an exclamation. The talk died, and I, turning from my corner, saw a very little old man standing behind the Rector's chair, motionless and smiling. He was one of the smallest men, not actually deformed, I have ever seen, small and very delicate looking. His white silky hair was thin on his head, but abundant over his ears; his face was like thin ivory, transparent and exquisitely carved; his eyes so over-hung that I could see nothing of them but two patches of shadow with a diamond in each. And there he stood, as if materialized from air, beneath the folds of his ample Roman cloak.

"I beg your pardon, reverend Fathers," he said—and his voice was as delicate as his complexion—"I tapped, but no one seemed to hear me."

The Rector bustled up from his chair.

"My dear Father—" he began, but Monsignor inter-rupted.

"A most appropriate entry, Father Girdlestone," he said. "You could not have made a more effective begin-ning." He moved his hand. "Father Girdlestone," he said, introducing us—"And this is the Father Rector."

We were all standing up by now, looking at this tran-quil little old man; and we bowed and murmured deferen-tially. There was something very dignified about this priest. Then chairs were re-sorted—I got my own again, moving it against the wall, watching him as, with almost foreign manners, he bowed this way and that before seating him-self in the centre. Then we all sat down; and after a word or two of talk, he began.

"I understand from my friend, Monsignor Maxwell," he said, "that you gentlemen would like to hear my story. I am very willing indeed to tell it. No possible harm can follow from it, and, perhaps even good may be the result, if ever anyone who shall hear it is afflicted with the same visitation. But it is a long story, gentlemen—and I am an old man and shall no doubt make it longer."

He was reassured, I think, by our faces, and without further apology he began his tale.

"My first and only curacy," he said, "was in the town of Cardiff. I was sent there after my ordination, four years before the re-establishment of the hierarchy in England; and the year after our bishops were given us I was sent to found a mission inland. Now, gentlemen, I shall not tell you where that was; though no doubt, you will be able to find out if you desire to do so. It will be enough now to describe to you the circumstances and the place.

"It was a little colliery village to which I went, we will call it Abergwyll. There was a number of Irish Catholics there—who are, as you know, the most devout persons on the face of the earth. They begged very hard for a priest, and, I suspect, gentlemen, there was collusion in the matter. The Bishop's chaplain had Irish blood in his veins."

He smiled pleasantly.

"At least, there I was sent, with a stipend of forty pounds and a letter of commendation and permission to beg. My parishioners set at my disposal a four-roomed house standing at the outskirts of the village, removed, I should say, forty yards from any other house. Behind my house was open country—a kind of moor—stretching over hill and dale to the mountains of Brecon. The colliery itself stood on the further side of the village and beneath it, half a mile away. Of the four rooms I used one as a chapel, on the ground floor; that at the back was the kitchen—I slept over the kitchen, and used as my sitting room and sacristy that over the chapel.

"I will not detain you with my first experiences. They were most edifying. I have never seen such devotion and fervour. My own devotion was sensibly increased by all that I heard and saw. The shepherd, in this case at least, was taught many lessons by his sheep.

"Now the first ambition of every young priest who is worthy of the name is to build a great church to God's glory. Even I had this ambition. I had not a great deal of work to do—in fact I may say that there was really nothing to do except to say mass and office, and to conduct evening devotions, as I did, every night in the chapel; and that little chapel, gentlemen, was full every night. Much of the day, therefore, I spent in walking and dreaming. In the morning, as summer came on, I was accustomed to take my office-book out with me, and to go over the moor, perhaps three hundred yards away, to a little ravine where a stream went down into the valley. There I would sit in the shade of a rock, listening to the voice of the water, and saying my prayers. When I had done I would lie on my back, looking up at the rock and the sky, and dreaming—well, as every young priest dreams.

"I do not know when it was that I first understood what God intended me to do. I began by thinking of a great town where my church should stand—Cardiff, or perhaps Newport. I even arranged its architecture; it was to be a primitive Roman basilica, large and plain, with a great apse with a Christ in glory frescoed there. On His right were to be the redeemed, on His left the lost—no more than that, with a pair of great angels behind the throne. That, gentlemen, without text or comment, has always seemed to me the greatest sermon on earth."

He paused, and looked round at us an instant.

"Well, gentlemen, you know what day-dreaming is. I even occupied my time—I—with forty pounds a year and thirty collier-parishioners—in drawing designs for my church. And then, suddenly, on a summer's day a new thought came to me, and something else with it.

"I was lying on my back on the short grass, looking up at the rock against the sky, when the thought came to me that here my basilica should stand. The rock should be levelled, I thought, to a platform. The foundations should be blasted out, and here my church should stand, alone on the moor, to witness that the demands of God's glory were dominant and sovereign… Yes, gentlemen, most unpractical and fantastic.…

"I sat up at the thought. It came to me as a revelation. In that instant I no more doubted that it should be accomplished than that God reigned. I looked below me at the stream. Yes, I saw it all; there the stream should dash and chatter; all about me were the solemn moors; and here, here on the rock behind me should stand my basilica, and the Blessed Sacrament within it.

"I was just about to turn to look at my rock again, when something happened."

The old man stopped dead.

"Now, gentlemen, I do not know if I can make this plain to you. What happened to me happened only interiorly, but it was as real as a thunder-clap or a vision. It was this—it was an absolute conviction that something was looking at me from over the top of the rock behind.

"My first thought was that I had heard a sound. Then simultaneously the horn blew from the colliery a mile away, and—and—" he hesitated, "I was aware that this external sound was on a different plane. I do not know how to make that plain to you; but it was as when one's imagination is full of some remembered melody and a real sound breaks upon it. The horn ceased and there was silence again. Then after a moment more my interior experience ceased too, as abruptly as it had begun.

"All that time, three or four seconds at least, I had sat still and rigid without turning my head. I must describe to you as well as I can my sensations during those seconds. You must forgive me for being verbose about it.

"Those who have attained to Saint Teresa's Prayer of Quiet tell us that it is a new world into which they consciously penetrate—a world with objects, sounds and all the rest—but that these are entirely incommunicable even to the brain of the percipient. No adequate image or analogy can be found for those intuitions; still less can they be expressed in words. I suppose that this is an illustration of the truth that the Kingdom of Heaven is within us.

"Well, gentlemen, I was aware during those seconds that I was in that state, that I had, as it were, stepped through the crust of the world of sense and even of intellectual thought. What I perceived of a person watching me was not on this plane at all. It was not one who in any sense had a human existence, who had ever had one, or ever would. It did not in the least resemble therefore an apparition of the dead. But the perception of this was gradual, as also of the nature of the visitation of which I shall speak in a moment. At first there was only the act of the entrance into my neighbourhood—as of one entering a room; then gradually, although with great speed, I perceived the nature of the visitation and the character of the visitant.

"And again, that sound, if I may call it so, was not that of a material object; it was not a cry or a word or a movement. Yet it was in some way the expression of a personality. Shall we say—" he stopped again. "Well, do you know what the sound of a flame is? There is not exactly a vibration—a note—nor a roar nor a—nor anything. Well, I do not think I can express it more clearly than by saying that that is the nearest analogy I can name in the world of sense. It was as the note of a vivid and intense personality; and it continued during that period and died noiselessly at the end like a sudden singing in the ears.

"Now I have taken the sense of hearing as the one which best expresses my experience; but it was not really hearing any more than seeing or tasting or feeling. It seemed to me that if it was true, as scientists tell us, that we have but one common sense expressing itself in five ways, that common sense was indirectly affected in this intense and piercing way only beneath its own plane, if I may say so.

"And one thing more. Although this presence seemed to bring on me a kind of paralysis, so that I did not move or even objectively think, yet beneath, my soul was aware of a repulsion and a hatred that I am entirely unable to describe. As God is absolute goodness and Love, so this presence affected me with precisely the opposite instinct.... There—I must leave it that. I must just ask you to take my word for it that there was present to me during those few seconds a kind of distilled quintessence of all that is Not-God, under the aspect of a person, and of a person, as I have said, quite apart from human existence."

The priest's quiet little voice, speaking now even lower than he began, yet perfectly articulate and unmoved, ceased; and I leaned back in my chair drawing a long breath. Again, I will only speak for myself, and say that he had seemed to be putting into words for the first time in my experience something which I had never undergone and which yet I recognized as simply true. I doubted it no more than if he had described a walk he had taken in Rome.

He looked round at the motionless faces; then he lifted one knee on to the other and began to nurse it.

"Well, gentlemen, it would be about ten minutes I suppose before I stood up. I looked over my shoulder before that, yet knowing I should see nothing, and indeed there was nothing to see but the old rock and the sky, and the silhouette of the grasses against it. I continued to sit there, because I felt too tired to move. It was a kind of complete languor that took possession of me. I had no actual fear now; I knew that the thing, whatever it was, had withdrawn itself—it had whisked, if I may say so, out of my range, as swift as a lizard who knows himself observed. I knew perfectly well that it would approach more cautiously if it should ever approach me again, but that for the present I need not fear.

"There was another curious detail too. I had—and have now—no reflex horror when I think of it. You see that it had not taken place before my senses—not even, indeed, before my intellect or my conscious powers. It was completely in the transcendent sphere; and therefore—at least I can only suppose that this is the reason—therefore when the door was shut, and I was returned to my human existence, I had no associations or even direct memory of the horror. I knew that it had taken place, but my objective imagination was not tarnished by it. Later, it was different; but I shall come to that presently. There was the languor, taking its rise I suppose in the very essence of my being where I had experienced and resisted the assault, and this languor communicated itself to my mind, just as weariness of mind communicates itself to the body. Then, after a little rest, I got up and went home. It was curious also that after dining the languor had risen even higher: I felt intolerably tired, and slept dreamlessly in my chair the whole afternoon.

"That then, gentlemen, was the beginning of my visitation. It was only the beginning, and to some degree differed from its continuation. It seemed to me, later, when I looked back upon it, that the personality had changed its assault somewhat, that at first it had rushed upon me unthinking, impelled by its own passion, and that afterwards it laid siege with skill and deliberation.... But are you sure, gentlemen, that I am not boring you with all this?"

Monsignor answered for us. (I noticed that he cleared his throat slightly before speaking.)

"No, no, Father…. Please go on."

The old priest paused a moment as if to recollect himself; then, still nursing his knee, he began again in his quiet little voice.

"I do not know exactly how long it was before I began to understand my danger; but I think the thought first occurred to me one day during my meditation. Soon after my ordination I had read Mme. Guyon's book on prayer, in order to understand exactly what it was that had been condemned in Quietism; and I suppose it had affected me to some extent. It is indeed a very subtle book, and extremely beautiful. At any rate I had long been accustomed to close my meditation with what she calls the "awful silence" in the Presence of God. I do not think that, normally speaking, there is any harm in this; on the contrary, for active-minded people in danger of intellectualism I think it a very useful exercise. Well, it was one day, I should think within a fortnight of my experience by the rock, that I first understood that for me there was danger. I was in my little chapel, before the Blessed Sacrament. Everything was quite quiet; the men were at work, and the women in their houses; it was a hot sunny morning I remember, breathlessly still. I had finished my formal meditation, and was sitting back in my chair.

"You all know, gentlemen, of course, the way in which one can approach the silence before God. Of course the simplest can do it if they will take pains."

Monsignor Maxwell interrupted, still in that slightly strained voice in which he had spoken just now.

"Please describe it," he said.

The priest looked up deprecatingly.

"Well, then. First, I had withdrawn myself from the world of sense. That takes, as you know, sometimes several minutes; it is necessary to sink down in thought in such a manner that sounds no longer distract the attention even though they may be heard, and even considered and reflected upon. Then the second step is to leave behind all intellectual considerations and images, and that too sometimes is troublesome, especially if the mind is naturally active. Well, this day I found an extraordinary ease in both the acts."

Father Brent leaned forward.

"May I interrupt, Father? But I am not sure that I understand,"

The old man pursed his lips. Then he glanced up at the rest of us almost apologetically.

"Well, it is this, my dear Father…. How can I put it? It is the introversion of the soul. Instead of considering this object or that, either by looking upon it or reflecting upon it, the soul turns inwards. There are the two distinct planes on which many men, especially those who pay little or no attention to the soul, live continually. Either they continually seek distractions; they cannot be devout except in company or before an image; or else—as indeed many do who have even the gift of recollection—they dwell entirely upon considerations and mental images. Now the true introversion is beneath all this. The soul sinks, turning inwards upon itself…there are no actual considerations at all; those become in their turn as much distractions to the energy of the soul as external objects to the energy of the mind…. Is that clearer, my dear Father?"

It was all said with a kind of patient and apologetic simplicity. Father Brent nodded pensively two or three times and dropped his chin again upon his hand. The old priest went on.

"Well, gentlemen, as I said just now, on this morning I came into the silence without an effort. First the sensible world dropped away. I heard a woman open and shut her door fifty yards away down the street; but it was no more than a sound. Then almost immediately the world of images and considerations went past me and vanished; and I found myself in perfect stillness.

"For an instant it seemed to me that all was well. There was that strange tranquillity all about me.… I cannot put it into words except by saying, as all do who practise that method, that it is a living tranquillity full of a very vital energy. This is not of course that to which contemplatives penetrate; St. John of the Cross makes that very plain; it is no more than that in which we ought always to live. It is that Kingdom of God within, of which our Blessed Lord tells us; but it is not the Palace itself.… However, as I have said, when one has but learnt the way there—and the difficulty of doing so lies only in its extreme and singular simplicity—when one has learnt the way there it is full of pleasure and consolation.

"I remained there, as my manner was, drawing a long breath or two as one is obliged to do—I do not know why. And at first all seemed well. There was that peace about me which may be described under the image of any one of the five senses. I prefer to speak of it now as under the image of light—a very radiant mellow light full of warmth and sweetness. There was too, just at first, that sense of profound abasement and adoration which is so familiar.… As I said, gentlemen, I do not of course for an instant pretend to the gift of pure contemplation; that is something far beyond.

"Then, all in an instant that sense of adoration vanished.

"Now it was not that I had risen back again to meditation; there were no images before my attention, no reflections of any formulated kind. It was still the pure perception, and yet all sense of adoration and of God's Majesty was gone. The light and the peace were there still, but—but not God.…

"Then I perceived, if I may say so, that something was on the point of disclosure. It was as if something was about to manifest itself. I perceived that the light was not as it had been. It was like that strange vivid sunlight that we see sometimes when a heavy cloud is overhead. That is the only way in which I can express it. It is for that reason that I called it *light*, rather than sound or touch. For an instant, still, I hesitated. The thought of what had happened to me by the rock never came to my mind; and with inconceivable swiftness the process passed on. To use an auditory metaphor for a moment it was like the change of an orchestra. The minor note steals in; a blight passes over the character of the sound; and, simultaneously the volume increases, the chords expand, tearing the heart with them; and the listener perceives that a moment later the climax will break in thunder."

He had raised his voice a little by now; his eyes glanced this way and that, though still without a trace of self-consciousness. Then again his voice dropped.

"Well, gentlemen, before that final moment came I had remembered. The vision of the rock and the chatter of the stream was before me, sharp as a landscape under lightning.… I do not know what I did; but I was aware of making a kind of terrified effort. My soul sprang up, as a diver who chokes under water; and in an instant the whole thing was gone. Then I became aware that my eyes were open, and that I was standing up. I was still terrified by the suddenness of the experience; and stood there, saying something aloud to our Lord in the Tabernacle. Then I heard the door open behind me.

"'Did you cry out, Father?' said Bridget, 'Why, Mother of Mercy!'

"I felt myself beginning to sway on my feet.… Well, gentlemen, I need not trouble you with all that. The truth was that Bridget, who was washing up my breakfast things in the kitchen, heard me cry out. She told me afterwards that when she saw my face she thought that I was dying.… I sat down a little then; and she fetched me something; and presently I was able to walk out.

"Well, gentlemen, that is enough for this evening."

He stopped abruptly.

We got up and went to night prayers.

2

"Well, so far," began Father Girdlestone on the following evening, "so far you see two things had happened to me. First there seems to have been a kind of unpremeditated assault that affected me body, mind and soul. That was the attack by the rock. Then he began to lay siege more deliberately, and attacked me in my meditation—in what I may call the innermost chamber—that ante room to the transcendent world. Now I have to tell you of his next assault."

There was a rustle of expectation as we settled ourselves to listen. I had found on questioning the others in the morning that they were in the same attitude as myself, impressed, but not convinced—indeed, strangely impressed by the extreme subtlety of the experience related to us. Yet there had been no proof, no tangible evidence, such as we are accustomed to demand, that the incidents had been anything more than subjective. At the same time there had been something remarkable in the priest's assurance as well as in the precise particularity of his narrative. It seemed now, however, from what he said, that perhaps we were to have more materialistic elements presented to us.

"The result, of course," continued Father Girdlestone, "of the attack upon my soul was that I became terrified at the thought of any further act of introversion. It seemed to me on reflection that I had probably overstrained my faculties a little, and that I had better be more distinctly meditative in devotion.

"I fetched down therefore from my shelves a copy of the *Spiritual Exercises*, and set to work. I began with a carefully objective act of thePresence of God, dwelling chiefly upon the Blessed Sacrament, and then pursued carefully the lines laid down. Two or three times every day, I should say, I was tempted to fall back upon the Prayer of Quiet; and each time I resisted it. It was a kind of frightened fascination that I felt for it. It was as if it had been a cupboard where something terrible lurked in silence and darkness, ready to tear me if I opened the door. Of course I should have opened it boldly—any priest of experience would have told me so at once—but I did not fully understand what was wrong. The result was as you shall hear.

"All went well for several days. I meditated with care, making the prescribed considerations—the preludes, the pictures and all the rest—observing to go straight from the intellectual act to the voluntary. I became soothed and content again. Then, without any warning the new assault was made. It came about in this fashion.

"I was meditating upon the Particular Judgment, and had formed the picture, as vividly as possible, of my soul before the Judge. I saw the wounds and the stains on one side; the ineffably piercing grace and holiness on the other. I saw the reproach in the Judge's face. I seized my soul by the neck, as it were, and crushed it down in humility and penitence. And then suddenly it seemed to me that my hold relaxed, and all faded. Now this assault came to me in intellectual form, yet I cannot remember the arguments. It began, if I may say so, as a blot upon the subject of my meditation, effacing the image of my Judge and of myself; and it spread with inconceivable swiftness over the whole of my faith...."

The priest paused, smiling steadily at the fire.

"How shall I put it?" he said. "Well, in a word it was intellectual doubt of the whole thing. A kind of cloud of infidelity seemed to envelop me. I beat against it; but it poured on, thick and black. There seemed to me no Person behind it; it was the very negative of Personality that surrounded me. 'After all,' it seemed to say to me, yet without words or intellect, you understand—'after all this is a pretty picture; but where is the proof? What shadow of a proof is there that the whole thing is not a dream? If there were objective proof, how could any man doubt? If there is not objective proof, what reason have you to trust in religion at all—far more to sacrifice your life to it? … Death, too— what is that but the resolving of the elements that issue in what you call the soul? And when the elements resolve the soul disperses,' and so on, and so on. You know it, gentlemen…. It suggested hostile things against our Lord when I turned to the Tabernacle. And then, on a sudden, as it had done in the deeper plane, it spread upwards to an intolerable climax. I began to see myself as a dying spark in a burning out world; and there was no escape—for there was nothing but empty space about me: no God, no heaven, not even a devil to hint at life in some form at least after death. I looked during those seconds into the gulf of annihilation…. I cried out in my heart that I would sooner live in hell than die there…and the vision, if I may call it so, of ultimate eternal blackness cleared every instant before my intellect until it was imminent upon me as a demonstrable certainty; and then, once more, before that loomed out as actually intellectually certain, I struggled, and stood up, saying something aloud, the name of God, I think, while the sweat poured down my face.

"It passed then—at least in its acuteness. There was the little domed Tabernacle before me with its white curtains, and the altar-cards and the gilt candlesticks; and a woman went past the window in clogs; and I heard a bird twitter beneath the eaves, and it was all, for a while, natural and peaceful again."

The priest stopped.

"Now, gentlemen," he said very slowly. "Intellectual difficulties have occurred to most people, I imagine. How should it not be so? If religion were small enough for our intellects it could not be great enough for our soul's requirements. But this was not just that fleeting transient obscurity that we call intellectual difficulty. It was to ordinary darkness, what substance is to imagination—what a visible concrete scene is to a fancy—what life is to dreaming. I know I cannot express what I mean; but I want you to take it on my word that this visitation in the realm of the intellect was a solid blackness, compared with which all other difficulties that I have ever heard of or experienced are as a mere lowering of intellectual lights. It was paralleled only by my experience in introversion. That, too, had not been an emotional withdrawal, or a spiritual dryness, as we commonly use those words. It had been a solid unutterably heavy burden—real beyond description.... And further, I want you to consider my dilemma. I had been routed in my soul and dared not take refuge there; I had been overwhelmed too, in my intellect; and even when the first misery had passed it seemed to me that the arguments against the Faith were stronger than those for it. I did not dare to put one against the other. A heavy deposit had been left upon my understanding. I did not dare to sit down and argue; I did not dare to run for refuge to the Silence of God. I was driven out into the sole thing that was left—the world of sense."

Again he stopped, still with that tranquil smile. I hardly understood him; though I think I saw very dimly what he had called his dilemma. Yet I did not understand what he meant by the "world of sense."

After a little pause he went on.

"To the world of sense," he repeated. "It seemed to me now that this was all that was left. I determined then and there to drop my meditation, and to confine myself to Mass, office, and rosary. I would say the words with my lips, quickly and steadily, keeping my mind fixed upon them rather than upon their meaning; and I would trust that presently the clouds would pass.

"Well, gentlemen, for about two months I continued this. The misery I suffered is simply indescribable. You can imagine all the suggestions I made to myself when I was off my guard. I told myself that I was a coward and a sham—that I had lost my faith and that I continued to act as a priest! What was especially hard to bear was the devotion of my parishioners. As I knelt in front saying the rosary and they responded, I could hear the thrill of conviction in every word that they uttered. Oh, those Irish! The things they said to me sometimes were like swords for pain…the Masses they asked me to say…

"I went to a priest at a distance once or twice and told him the bare outline—not as I have told it to you. He laughed at me, kindly of course. He told me that it was the effect of loneliness, while I knew that at the best it was the work of one who bore me continual company now and who was stronger than I. He told me that all young priests had to win the victory in some form or other; that every priest thought his own case the most desperate…. Yet I knew from every word that he said that he did not understand, and that I could never make him understand. Yet, somehow, I set my teeth: I told God that I was willing to bear this dereliction for as long as He willed—so paradoxical and mysterious is the gift of Faith—if He would but save my soul; and at last, in a kind of defiance, I began to look once more at my designs for the church I was to build.

"You see, gentlemen, what I meant by taking refuge in the world of sense. I deliberately contemplated never daring to face God again interiorly, or even my own soul. I would do my duty as a priest; I would say my Mass and office; I would preach strictly what the Church enjoined; I would live and die like that, with my teeth set. Better God beaten and denied, than all the world beside in prosperity!"

For the first time in the whole of his narrative Father Girdlestone's voice trembled a little. He passed his thin old hand over his mouth once or twice, shifted his position and began again.

"It was on the first of October that I took down my plans again. I had not looked at them for two months: I had not the heart to do so.

"Now let me describe to you exactly the room in which I sat and the other necessary circumstances.

"In the centre of my room stood my table with two windows on my left, the fire in front and the door behind me to the right. The windows were hung with serge curtains. I had no carpet; but a little mat only beneath my table and another before the fire.

"It was in the beginning of October—to be accurate, the third of the month—that this thing happened that I am about to tell you.

"I awoke early that morning, said my Mass as usual, with attention and care, but no sensible devotion, and after my thanksgiving sat down to breakfast. It was then that I first had any uneasiness.

"I was breakfasting at my table, and beyond me, in front and to the right stood a large basket chair. I was reading some book or other, and can honestly say that nothing was further from my mind than my experiences in the summer. Remember, during two months nothing had happened— nothing at least, beyond that intolerable intellectual dark- ness. Then the basket-chair suddenly clicked, in the way in which they do half an hour after one has sat in them. It distracted my attention for an instant—it was just enough for that, no more. I went on with my book.

"Then it clicked again, three or four times; and I looked up, rather annoyed.... Well, to be brief, this went on and on. After breakfast when Bridget came to fetch the tray I asked whether she had touched the chair that morning. She told me no. (All this time, remember, no thought of anything odd had entered my head.) I supposed it was the damp, and said so.

"While she was still in the room I went out to fetch my breviary from the chapel; and as I set foot on the stairs, leaving the door open behind me, I heard her, as I thought, come out after me with the tray, and follow me, three or

four steps behind, all down the staircase. I had no more
doubt of that than of the fact that I myself was going down-
stairs. At the turn of the stairs I did not even look behind.
By the sounds—not clear footfalls you understand—but a
kind of shuffling and breathing, and still more by the con-
sciousness that there she was, I judged she was in a hurry,
as she often was. At the foot of the stairs I turned to say
something, and, as I began to turn I will swear that I saw
a figure out of the corner of my eye; but when I looked, it
was simply not there. There was nothing there.... Do you
understand, gentlemen? Nothing at all.

"I called up to her, and heard her come across the floor.
Then she looked over the banister.

"'Did you come out of the room just now?' I said.

"'No, your Reverence.'

"Well, I made my theory of course. It was to the effect
that she had moved in the room as I came out, that I there-
fore thought she was following me, and that the rest was
simply self-suggestion.

"I got my breviary and came out. As I came into the
little lobby, again there occurred to me the impression that
someone was there, waiting in the corner. I looked round
me: there was nothing—and I went upstairs.

"Gentlemen, do you know that nervous condition
when one feels there is someone in the room? It is gener-
ally dissipated in ten minutes' conversation. Well, I was in
that condition all the morning. But there was more than
that.

"It was not only that sense of someone there; there
were sounds now and then, very faint, but absolutely

distinct, coming from all quarters—sounds so minute and unimportant in themselves that I might have heard them a hundred times without giving them another thought, if they had not been accompanied by that sense of a presence with me. They were of all kinds. Once or twice a piece of woodwork somewhere in the room clicked, as my basket-chair had done—a sharp minute rap such as one hears in damp weather. Once the door became unlatched and slid very softly with the sound of a hush over a piece of matting that lay there. I got up and shut the door again, looking, I must confess, for an instant on to the landing; and as I came back to my chair, that clicked twice.

"Gentlemen, I know this sounds absurd. You will be saying, as I said, that I was simply in a nervous condition. Very well, perhaps I was: but please wait. Once, as I sat in my chair drawn sideways near the fireplace a very slight movement caught my eye. I turned sharply; it was no more than the fringe of the mat under the table fitting in the draught. As I looked it ceased.

"Well, my nerves got worse and worse. I stared every now and then round the room. There was nothing to be seen but the boards, the mats, the familiar furniture, the black and white crucifix over the mantelshelf, my few books, and the vestment-chest near the door. There were the curtains, too, hanging at the windows. That was all. It was a cloudy October day; and rained a little about half-past twelve. I remember starting suddenly as a gust came and dashed the drops against the glass.

"At about a quarter to one, Bridget came in to lay dinner.... I am ashamed to say it, but I was extraordinarily relieved when I heard her open the downstairs door. (She came in, you remember, three or four times a day to see after me; otherwise I was alone in the house.)

"When she came into the room I looked up at her.… She smiled at me, and then it seemed to me that her face took on it rather an odd expression. She stopped smiling, and before she set down the tablecloth and knives she looked round the room rather curiously, I thought.

"'Well, Bridget,' I said, 'what is it?'

"There was just a moment before she answered.

"'It is nothing, your Reverence,' she said.

"Then she laid dinner. I dined, reading all the while, and she brought in the dishes one by one. I am afraid I hurried rather over dinner. I made up my mind to go out for a long walk; there was something else in my mind too—well—I may as well tell you—it seemed to me that I should rather like to be out of the house before she was. Yes, it was cowardly; but remember that all this while I was telling myself that I had an attack of the nerves, and that I had better not be alone except in the fresh air.

"Well, nothing at all happened that afternoon. It seemed to me as I went over the moors that all sense of haunting had ceased; I noticed first consciously that it had gone soon after leaving the outskirts of the village; I was entirely happy and serene.

"As I came back into sight of the village at dusk, and saw the lights shining over the hill, the uneasiness came on me again. It struck me vividly for the first time that a night spent alone in that house would be slightly uncomfortable. By this time, of course, too, the possibility of a connexion between my present state and my other experiences had occurred to my mind; but I had striven to resist this idea as merely one more nervous suggestion.

"My uneasiness grew greater still as I came up the street. I am ashamed to say that I stopped to talk three or four times to my parishioners simply out of that unaccountably strong terror of my own house. I noticed too, across the street that a face peeped from Bridget's window and drew back on seeing me. A moment later the door opened and she came out.

"I did not turn or wait for her; but as I reached my door I was conscious of a very distinct relief that she was behind me, and as I went in she came immediately after me.

"'I am very sorry, Father,' she said, 'I haven't your tea ready yet.'

"I told her to bring it as soon as she could, and went slowly upstairs with the horror deepening at every step. I knew perfectly well now why she had waited: it was that she did not like to enter the empty house alone.... Yet I did not feel that I could ask her what it was that she feared. That would be a kind of surrender on my part—an allowing to myself that there was something to fear; and you must remember that I still was trying to tell myself that it was all nerves."

The Rector leaned forward.

"I am very sorry, Father Girdlestone," he said softly; "but it is past time for night prayers." He paused. "But may we make an exception tonight, and hear the rest afterwards?"

The old man stood up, and motioned with a little smile towards the chapel gallery.

3

"As I went forward into the room," began the old man again, as soon as we had taken our seats in silence, "I knew beyond doubt that I was accompanied. I heard Bridget moving about downstairs; but it was as sound heard through the roar of a train. There went with me something resembling a loud noise—interior, you understand, yet on the brink of manifestation in the world of sense—or you may call it a blackness, or a vast weight as heavy as heaven and earth—and it was all centred round a personality. It was of such a nature that I should have been surprised at nothing. It appeared to me that all that I looked upon— the serge curtains, my table, my chair, the glow of the fire on the hearth and the glimmer on the bare boards—all these were but as melting shreds and rags hanging upon some monstrous reality. They were there—they were just in existence; but they were as accidents without substance.

"I do not know if there were definite sounds or not— or even definite appearances—beyond the normal material sounds and sights. There may have been; but I do not think so.

"I went across the room, walking, it seemed to me, on nothingness. My body was still in sensible relations with matter, but it seemed to me that I was not. I found my chair and sat down in it to wait. I was nerveless now, sunk in a kind of despair that I cannot hope to make plain to you. I imagine that a lost soul on the edge of death must be in that state.

"I looked almost vacantly round the room once or twice; but there was nothing. I understood without consideration what was happening, and the general course of events. It was all one, I perceived now. That which had started up at the rock—which had invaded first the innermost chamber of my soul, and then the intellectual plane, and had established itself there, had now taken its final step forward, and was claiming the world of sense as well. I felt entirely powerless. You will wonder why I did not go downstairs to the Blessed Sacrament—I do not know; but it was impossible. Here was the battlefield, I knew very well.

"I perceived something else too. It was the reason of the assaults. I did not fully understand it; but I knew that the object was to drive me from the place—to make the village and neighbourhood detestable to me. I knew that I could escape by going away; yet it was not exactly a temptation—I had no interior desire to escape. It was merely a question as to which force would prevail in my soul—that which impelled me away, and grace which held me there. I was as a passive dummy between them.

"I do not know how long it was before Bridget pushed open the door. I saw her with the tray come across the room and set it down upon my table. Then I saw her looking at me.

"'Bridget,' I said, 'I shall want no supper tonight. And tell the people that I am unwell and that there will be no night prayers. There will be Mass, I hope, as usual, in the morning.'

"I said these words, I believe; but the voice was not as my own, it was as if another spoke. I saw her looking at me across the dusk with an extraordinary terror in her face.

"'Come away, Father,' she whispered.

"I shook my head.

"'Come away,' she whispered again; 'this is not a good house to be in.'

"I said nothing.

"'Shall I fetch Father Donovan to you, Father,' she whispered, 'or the doctor?'

"'Fetch no one,' I said to her. 'Tell no one—ask for prayers, if you will. Go and leave me to myself, Bridget.'

"I think I understood even then what the struggle was she was going through. I do not know if she perceived all that I perceived; but even from her face, without her words, I knew that she was conscious of something. Yet she did not like to leave me alone. She stood perfectly still, looking first at me, then slowly round the room; then back at me again. And as she looked the dusk fell veil on veil.

"Then something happened: I do not know what; I never questioned her afterwards; but she was gone; I heard her stumbling and moaning down the stairs. An instant later the street door opened and banged, and I was left alone.

"I cannot tell you what I felt. I knew only that the crisis was come, and that the result was out of my hands. I closed my eyes, I think, and lay right back in my chair. It was as if I was submitting myself to an operation; I wondered vaguely as to what shape it would take.

"All about the room I felt the force gathering. There was no oscillation, no vibration, but a steady continuous pressure concentrating itself within the four walls. With this the sense of the central personality grew every moment more and more intense and vivid. It seemed to me as if I were some tiny conscious speck of matter in the midst of a life whose vastness and malignance was beyond conception. At times it was this; at other times it was as if I looked within and saw a space full of some indescribable blackness—a space of such a nature that I could not tell whether it was as tiny as a pinhole or as vast as infinity. It was spaceless space, sheer emptiness, but with an emptiness that was a horror; and it was within me.

"Yet it was not simple spirit—it was not the correlative of matter. It was rather spirit in the very throes of manifestation in matter.

"Sometimes then I attended to this; sometimes I lay with every sense at full stretch—at a tenseness that seemed impossible, directed outwards. I cannot tell even now whether the room was poised in deathly silence, or in an indescribable clamour and roar of tongues. It was one or the other; or it was both at once.

"Or to take the sense of sight. Although my eyes were closed every detail of the room was before me. Sometimes I saw it as rigid as a man at grips with death, in a kind of pallor—the table, the dying fire, the uncurtained windows all in the pallor—the very names of the books visible—all, as it were, striving to hold themselves in material being under the stress of some enormous destructive force with which they were charged—as rigid and as silent and

as significant as an electric wire—and as full of power. Or
at times all seemed to me to have gone, simply to have dis-
solved into nothingness, as a breath fades on a window—to
retain but a phantom of themselves.

"Well, well—words are very useless, gentlemen; they
are poor things—"

The old priest paused a moment, leaning forward in
his chair with his thin veined hands together. For myself
I cannot say what I felt. I seemed to be in somewhat of
the state as that which he was describing: all my senses
too were stretched to the full by the intensity of my atten-
tion. Yet the narrator seemed little affected; he leaned and
looked peacefully into the fire, and I caught the glint of
light on his deep eyes. Then he leaned back, and went on.

"Now you must picture to yourselves, gentlemen,
that this state grew steadily in its energy. I did not know
before—and I can scarcely believe it now—that human
nature could bear so much. Yet I seemed to myself to be
observing my strained faculties from a plane apart from
them. It was as the owner of a besieged castle might stand
on a keep and watch the figures of his men staring out over
the battlements at a sight he could not see. There were my
eyes looking, my ears listening, even the touch of my fin-
gers on the chair arms questioning what it was that they
held; and there was I—my very self—far within waiting for
communications.

"I suppose that I knew there was no escape. I could
not descend into the sphere of reason, for another power
held the keys; I could not sink again to the inner presence
of God, for that chamber too was occupied; there was this

last stand to be made—the world of sense. If that was lost, all was lost, and I could not lift a finger to help. And, as I said, the strain grew greater each instant, as the opening swell of an organ waxes with a long steady crescendo to its final roar.

"I do not know at exactly what point I understood the assault, but it became known to me presently that what was intended was to merge the world of sense, so far as I was concerned, into this mighty essence of evil—to burst through, or rather to transcend the material. Then, I knew, I should be wholly lost. I remember too that I perceived soon after this that this was what the world calls madness. And I understood at this moment, as never before, how that process consummates itself. It begins, as mine did, with the carrying of the inner life by storm; that may come about by deliberate acquiescence in sin—I should suppose that it always does in some degree. Then the intellect is attacked—it may only be in one point—a 'delusion' it is called; and with many persons regarded only as eccentric the process goes no further. But when the triumph is complete, the world of sense too is lost—and the man raves. I knew at that time for absolute fact that this is the process. The 'delusions' of the mad are not non-existent—they are glimpses, horrible or foul or fantastic, of that strange world that we take so quietly for granted, that at this moment and at every moment is perpetually about us—foaming out its waters in lust or violence or mad irresponsible blasphemy against the Most High.

"Well, I saw that this was what threatened; yet I could not move a finger. No thought of flight entered my mind.

All had gone too far by now.

"Then, gentlemen, the climax came."

Again the old priest was silent.

I heard Monsignor's pipe drop with a clatter; and my nerves thrilled like a struck harp. He made no movement to pick it up. He stared only at the old man.

Then the quiet voice went on.

"This was the climax, gentlemen. The intensity swelled and swelled—each moment I thought must be the last— the utmost effort of hell. Then with a crash the full close sounded; and through the rending tear—through the veil of matter that whirled away and was gone—I caught one swift glimpse of all that lay beneath. It was not through one sense that I perceived it; it was through perception pure and simple. Well—how can I say it? It was this. I perceived two vast forces pressed one against the other, as silent and as rigid as—as the glass of a diver's helmet against the huge incumbent glimmering water. It is a wretched simile—let us say that the appearance was as the meeting of fire and water without mist or tumult. The forces were absolutely opposed—absolutely alien—yet absolutely one in the plane of being. They could meet as the created and uncreated could not—as flesh and spirit cannot. They met, level, coincident—each rigid to breaking point—each full of an energy to which there is no parallel in this world.

"It seemed to me that all had waited for this. The enemy had been permitted to stand in the gate, and at the instant of his triumph the fire of God was upon him, locked in the embrace of utter repulsion.

"And it was given to me to watch that, gentlemen. On

the edge of what the world labels as madness, at the very instant that I hung balanced on that line, I saw that endless war of spirit and spirit which has been raging since Michael drove Satan from heaven—that ceaseless untiring conflict in which all that is not for God is against Him, seeking to dethrone and annihilate Him who gave it being. Ah, words—words—but I saw it."

There was a dead silence in the room. The priest drew one breath.

"Then I saw no more. I was in my chair as before, holding the arms, and the room round me stole back into being—through the pallor of a phantom, to the dusk of earthly twilight—and I perceived that my eyes were closed and not open.

"There then I stayed, knowing that the war still raged beneath, yet fainter every moment as the tide crawled back, contesting inch by inch, rolled back by that remorseless power. Twice or three times I heard the murmur of sound in the room; the serge curtains swayed—I could hear them—I heard the door vibrating softly: then once more the quiet silence was there, and I heard the ashes slip by their weight from grate to fender. Matter at last was itself again; then once more, as into my intellect the light stole back, and I knew that God reigned and that His Son was incarnate, crucified and risen by many eirrefragable proofs, round the house I could hear the murmuring of voices, and see through closed eye-lids of utter repose the glimmer of lanterns on the ceiling.

"Within myself too I watched the rout of evil; I drew breath after breath, deep and life-giving, as far down within the secret chambers of my soul the foul filth ebbed and sank and that spring rising into life everlasting, of which our Saviour spoke, welled up in its stead, filling every cranny and corner of my soul with that strange sweetness, so sweet and so dear that we forget it as the very air we breathe. The murmur of conflict was infinitely far away; and it seemed to me that once more I went down, down, in that introversion of which I spoke just now, seeing all clean and sweet about me, down into the presence of the Lord who rules Heaven and earth at His will. Then a door closed, deep, deep below; and I knew that the enemy was gone."

"Well, gentlemen," said the priest after a pause, leaning back, "that is really the story. But there are a few details to add.

"When the men that Bridget had fetched came upstairs, they found me asleep; but, they told me afterwards, there were streaks of foam at the corners of my mouth. Yet she was not gone three minutes.

"I never spoke a word to them of what happened—they knew quite enough for laymen. We had night prayers as usual that evening. I said the *Visita quaesumus Domine* at the end.

"I slept like a child; and I said a mass of thanksgiving next day."

Father Brent broke the silence that followed. His voice seemed strange.

"And the church, Father?"

The old priest smiled at him full.

"You have guessed it," he said. "Yes: the church was built thirty years later. It is a basilica, as I said; it presents our Lord in glory in an apse. It stands curiously enough on the rock; but it is in the middle of a huge colliery town— and—well, I may as well say it—there is a grated tribune above the high altar at one side, through which a convent of Poor Clares can assist at the Holy Sacrifice. Poor Clares! I ceased to wonder at the assault as soon as the convent was built."

He stood up smiling.

VI

Father Bianchi's Story

FATHER Bianchi, as the days went on, seemed a little less dogmatic on the theory that miracles (except of course those of the saints) did not happen. He was warned by Monsignor Maxwell that his turn was approaching to contribute a story; and suddenly at supper he announced that he would prefer to get it over at once that evening.

"But I have nothing to tell," he cried, expostulating with hands and shoulders, "nothing to tell but the nonsense of an old peasant woman."

When we had taken our places upstairs, and the Italian had again apologized and remonstrated with raised eyebrows, he began at last; and I noticed that he spoke with a seriousness that I should not have expected.

"When I was first a priest," he said, "I was in the south of Italy, and said my first Mass in a church in the hills. The village was called Arripezza."

"Is that true?" asked Monsignor suddenly, smiling.

The Italian grinned brilliantly. "Well, no," he said, "but it is near enough, and I swear to you that the rest is true. It was a village in the hills, ten miles from Naples. They have many strange beliefs there; it is like Father Brent's Cornwall. All along the coast, as you know, they set lights in the windows on one night of the year; because they relate that Our Lady once came walking on the water with her Divine Child, and found none to give her shelter. Well, this village that we will call Arripezza was not on the coast. It was inland, but it had its own superstitions to compensate it—superstitions cursed by the Church.

"I knew little of all this when I went there. I had been in the seminary until then.

"The *parrocho* was an old man, but old! He could say Mass sometimes on Sundays and feasts, but that was all, and I went to help him. There were many at my first Mass, as the custom is, and they all came up to kiss my hands when it was done.

"When I came back from the sacristy again there was an old woman waiting for me, who told me that her name was Giovannina. I had seen her before, as she kissed my hands. She was as old as the *parrocho* himself—I cannot tell how old—yellow and wrinkled as a monkey.

"She put five lire into my hands.

"'Five Masses, Father,' she said, 'for a soul in purgatory.'

"'And the name?'

"'That does not matter,' she said, 'and will you say them, my Father, at the altar of S. Espedito?'

"I took the money and went off, and as I went down the church I saw her looking after me, as if she wished to speak, but she made no sign and I went home; and I had a dozen other Masses to say, some for my friends, and a couple that the *parrocho* gave me, and those, therefore, I began to say first. When I had said the fifth of the twelve, Giovannina waited for me again at the door of the sacristy. I could see that she was troubled.

"'Have you not said them, my Father?' she asked. 'He is here still.'

"I did not notice what she said, except the question, and I said no, I had had others to say first. She blinked at me with her old eyes a moment, and I was going on, but she stopped me again.

"'Ah! Say them at once, Father,' she said; 'he is waiting.'

"Then I remembered what she had said before, and I was angry.

"'Waiting!' I said. 'And so are thousands of poor souls.'

"'Ah, but he is so patient,' she said; 'he has waited so long.'

"I said something sharp, I forget what, but the *parrocho* had told me not to hang about and talk nonsense to women, and I was going on, but she took me by the arm.

"'Have you not seen him too, my Father?' she said.

"I looked at her, thinking she was mad, but she held me by the arm and blinked up at me, and seemed in her senses. I told her to tell me what she meant, but she would not. At last I promised to say the Masses at once. The next morning I began the Masses, and said four of them, and at each the old woman was there close to me, for I said them at the altar of S. Espedito, that was in the nave, as she had asked me, and I had a great devotion to him as well, and she was always at her chair just outside the altar-rails. I scarcely saw her, of course, for I was a young priest and had been taught not to lift my eyes when I turned round, but on the fourth day I looked at her at the *Orate fratres,* and she was staring not at me or the altar, but at the corner on the left. I looked there when I turned, there was nothing but the glass-case with the silver hearts in it to S. Espedito.

"That was on a Friday, and in the evening I went to the church again to hear confessions, and when I was done, the old woman was there again.

"'They are nearly done, my Father,' she said, 'and you will finish them tomorrow?'

"I told her yes, but she made me promise that whatever happened I would do so.

"Then she went on, 'Then I will tell you, my Father, what I would not before. I do not know the man's name, but I see him each day during Mass at that altar. He is in the corner. I have seen him there ever since the church was built.'

"Well, I knew she was mad then, but I was curious about it, and asked her to describe him to me; and she did so. I expected a man in a sheet or in flames or something of the kind, but it was not so. She described to me a man in a dress she did not know—a tunic to the knees, bareheaded, with a short sword in his hand. Well, then I saw what she meant—she was thinking of S. Espedito himself. He was a Roman soldier, you remember, gentlemen?

"'And a cuirass?' I said. 'A steel breastplate and helmet?'

"Then she surprised me.

"'Why, no, Father, he has nothing on his head or breast, and there is a bull beside him!'

"Well, gentlemen, I was taken aback by that. I did not know what to say."

Monsignor leaned swiftly forward.

"Mithras," he said abruptly.

The Italian smiled.

"Monsignor knows everything," he said.

Then I broke in, because I was more interested than I knew.

"Tell me, Monsignor, what was Mithras?"

The priest explained shortly. It was an Eastern worship, extraordinarily pure, introduced into Italy a little after the beginning of the Christian. Mithras was a god, filling a position not unlike that of the Second Person of the Blessed Trinity. He offered a perpetual sacrifice, and through that sacrifice souls were enabled to rise from earthly things to heavenly, if they relied upon it and accompanied that faith by works of discipline and prayer. It was one of those shadows of reality, said the Canon, of which pagan religions are so full.

"I beg your pardon, Father Bianchi," he ended.

The Italian smiled again.

"Yes, Monsignor," he said, "I know that now, but I did not know it for many years afterwards, and I know something else now that I did not know then. Well, to return.

"I told my old woman that she was dreaming, that it could not be so, that there was no room for a bull in the corner, that it was a picture of S. Espedito that she was thinking of.

"'And why did you not get the Masses said before?' I asked.

"She smiled rather slyly at me then.

"'I did get five said once before,' she said, 'in Naples, but they did him no good. And when once again I told the *parrocho* here, he told me to be off; he would not say them.'

"And she had waited for a young priest, it seemed, and

had determined not to tell him the story till the Masses were said, and had saved up her money meanwhile.

"Well, I went home, and got to talking with the old priest, and led him on, so that he thought that he had introduced the subject, and presently he told me that when the foundation of the church had been laid, forty years before, they had found an old cave in the hill, with heathen things in it. He knew no more than that about it, but he told me to fetch a bit of pottery from a cupboard, and he showed it me, and there was just the tail of a bull upon it, and an eagle."

Monsignor leaned forward again.

"Just so," he said, "and the bull was lying down."

The Italian nodded, and was silent.

We all looked at him. It seemed a tame ending I thought. Then Father Brent put our thoughts into words.

"That is not all? "he said.

Father Bianchi looked at him sharply, and at all of us, but said nothing.

"Ah, that is not all!" said the other again, persistently.

"Bah!" cried the Italian suddenly. "It was not all, if you will have it so. But the rest is madness, as mad as Giovanni-na herself. What I saw, I saw because she made me expect it. It was nothing but the shadow, or the light in the glass case."

A perceptible thrill ran through us all. The abrupt change from contempt to seriousness was very startling.

"Tell us, Father," said the English priest, "we shall think no worse of you for it. If it was only the shadow, what harm is there in telling it?"

"Indeed you must finish," went on Monsignor; "it is in the contract."

The Italian looked round again, frowned, smiled, and laughed uneasily.

"I have told it to no one till today," he said, "but you shall hear it. But it was only the shadow—you understand that?"

A chorus, obviously insincere, broke out from the room.

"It was only the shadow, Padre Bianchi."

Again the priest laughed shortly; the smile faded, and he went on.

"I went down early the next morning, before dawn, and I made my meditation before the Blessed Sacrament; but I could not help looking across once or twice at the corner by S. Espedito's altar; it was too dark to see anything clearly, but I could make out the silver hearts in the glass case. When I had finished, Giovannina came in.

"I could not help stopping by her chair as I went to rest.

"'Is there anything there?' I asked.

"She shook her head at me.

"'He is never there till Mass begins,' she said.

"The sacristy door that opens out of doors was set wide as I came past it in my vestments; and the dawn was coming up across the hills, all purple."

Monsignor murmured something, and the priest stopped.

"I beg your pardon," said Monsignor, "but that was the time the sacrifice of Mithras was offered."

"When I came out into the church," went on the priest, "it was all grey in the light of the dawn, but the chapels were still dark. I went up the steps, not daring to look in the corner, and set the vessels down. As I was spreading the corporal, the server came up and lighted the candles. And still I dared not look. I turned by the right and came down, and stood waiting till he knelt beside me.

"Then I found I could not begin. I knew what folly it was, but I was terribly frightened. I heard the server whisper, *In nomine Patris*....

"Then I shut my eyes tight, and began.

"Well, by the time I had finished the preparation, I felt certain that something was watching me from the corner. I told myself, as I tell myself now," snapped the Italian fiercely, "I told myself it was but what the woman had told me. And then at last I opened my eyes to go up the steps— but I kept them down; and only saw the dark corner out of the side of my eyes.

"Then I kissed the altar and began.

"Well, it was not until the Epistle that I understood that I should have to face the corner at the reading of the Gospel; but by then I do not think I could have faced it directly, even if I had wished.

"So when I was saying the *Munda cor* in the centre, I thought of a plan; and as I went to read the Gospel I put my left hand over my eyes, as if I was in pain, and read the Gospel like that. And so all through the Mass I went on; I always dropped my eyes when I had to turn that way at all; and I finished everything and gave the blessing.

"As I gave it, I looked at the old woman, and she was

kneeling there, staring across at the corner, so I knew that she was still dreaming she saw something.

"Then I went to read the Last Gospel."

The priest was plainly speaking with great difficulty; he passed his hands over his lips once or twice. We were all quiet.

"Well, gentlemen—courage came to me then, and as I signed the altar I looked straight into the corner."

He stopped again, and began resolutely once more, but his voice rang with hysteria.

"Well, gentlemen, you understand that my head was full of it now, and that the corner was dark, and the shadows were very odd."

"Yes, yes, Padre Bianchi," said Monsignor, easily, "and what did the shadows look like?"

The Italian gripped the arms of the chair, and screamed his answer:

"I will not tell you, I will not tell you. It was but the shadow. My God, why have I told you the tale at all?"

VII

Father Jenks' Tale

I have not yet had occasion to describe Father Jenks, the Ontario priest: partly, I think, because he had not previously distinguished himself by anything but silence, and partly because he was so true to his type that I had scarcely noticed even that.

It was not until the following evening, when he was seated in the central chair of the group, that I really observed him sufficiently to take in his characteristics with any definiteness and to see how wholly he was American. He was clean-shaven; with a heavy mouth, square jaw, and an air of something that I must call dulness, relieved only by a spark of alertness in each of his eyes, as he leaned back and began his story. He spoke deliberately, in an even voice, and as he spoke looked steadily a little above the fire; his hands lay together on his right knee which was crossed over his left; and I noticed a large elastic-sided boot cocked toward the warmth. I knew that he had passed a great part of his early life in England; and I was not surprised to observe that he spoke with hardly a trace of American accent or phraseology.

"I, too, am a man of one story," he said. "I dare say you may think it not worth the telling. But it impressed me."

He looked round with heavy, amused eyes as if to apologize.

"It was when I was in England in the eighties. I was in the Cotswolds. You know them perhaps?"

Again he looked round. Monsignor Maxwell jerked the ash off his cigarette impatiently. This American's air of leisure was a little tiresome.

"I lived in a cottage," went on the other, "at the edge of Minchester, not two hundred yards from the old church. My own schism shop, as the parson called it once or twice in the local paper, was a tin building behind my house—it was not beautiful. It was a kind of outlandish stranger beside the church; and the parson made the most of that. I never was able to understand—"

He broke off again, and pressed his lips in a reminiscent smile.

"Now all that part of the Cotswolds is like a table: it is flat at the top with steep sides sloping down into the valleys. The great houses stand mostly halfway down these slopes. It is too windy on the top for their trees and gardens. The Dominicans have a house a few miles from Minchester, up one of the opposite hills, and I would go across there to my confession on Saturday, and stay an hour or two over tea, talking to one of them. It was there that I heard the tale of the house I am going to speak about.

"This was a house that stood not two miles from my own village—a great place, built halfway down one of the slopes. It had been a Benedictine house once, though there was little enough of that part left; most of it was red-brick with twisted chimneys, but on the lawn that sloped down toward the wood and the stream at the bottom of the valley there was the west arch of the nave still standing with the doorway beneath and a couple of chapels on either side. Mrs.—er—Arbuthnot we will call her, if you please—had laid it out with a rockery beneath; and once I saw her, from the hill behind, drinking tea with her friends in one of the chapels.

"Then the dining room, I heard from the Dominicans, had been the abbot's chapel. This, too, was what they told me. The house had been shut up for forty years, and had a bad name. It had once been a farm, but things had happened there: the sons had died; a famous horse bred there had broken its neck somehow on the lawn. Then another family had taken it from the owner, and the only son of the lot too had died; and then folks began to talk about a curse; and the oldest inhabitant was trotted out as usual to make mischief and gossip; and the end was the house was shut up.

"Then the owner had built on to it. He pulled down a bit more of the ruins, meaning to live in it himself, and then his son went up."

The Canadian smiled with one corner of his mouth.

"This is what I heard from the Dominicans, you know."

Father Brent looked up swiftly.

"They are right though," he said. "I know the house and others like it."

"Yes, Father," said the other priest. "Your island has its points."

He recrossed his legs and drew out his pipe and pouch.

"Well, as this priest says, there are other houses like it. Otherwise I could scarcely tell this tale. It's too ancient and feudal to happen in my country."

He paused so long to fill his pipe that Father Maxwell sighed aloud.

"Yes, Monsignor," said the priest without looking up. "I am going on immediately."

He put his pipe into the corner of his mouth, took out his matches, and went on.

"Well, Mrs. Arbuthnot had taken the house a year before I came to Minchester. She was what the Dominicans called a frivolous woman; but I called her real solid before the end. What they meant was that she had parties down there and tea in the chapel, and a dresser with blue plates where the altar used to stand in the abbot's time, and a vestment for her fire-screen, and all that; and a couple of chestnuts that she used to drive about the country with, and a groom in boots, and a couple of fellows with powdered hair to help her in and out.

"Well, I saw all that at a garden party she gave, and I must say we got on very well. I had seen her before once or twice out of my window on Sunday morning going along with a morocco prayer-book with a cross on it, and a bonnet on the back of her head. Then I showed her round the old church one day with some visitors of hers, and she left a card on me next day.

"On the day of the garden party I saw the house, and the blue china and the rest, and she asked me what I thought of it all, and I said it was very nice; and she asked me whether I thought it wrong, with a sort of cackle, and I told her she had better follow her own religious principles and let me follow mine, and not have any exchanges. She told me then I was a sensible man, and she called up her son to introduce us. He was a fellow of twenty or so, a bright lad, up at Oxford. He was just engaged to be married, too—that was why they had the party; and when I saw his girl, I thought things looked pretty unwholesome for the old house, and I think I said so to the old lady. She thought me more sensible than ever after that, and I heard her telling another old body what I had said."

The Canadian paused again to strike a match; and I saw the corners of his mouth twitching, either with the effort to draw, or with amusement—I scarcely knew which. When the pipe was well alight, he went on:

"It was on the last Sunday of September that year that I heard the young man was ill and that the marriage was put off. I remember it well, partly because they were having a high time at the church, decorating it all for Michaelmas, which was next day, with the parson pretending it was for Harvest Festival, as they always do. I had seen the pumpkins go in the day before, and wondered where they put them all. I went up to the churchyard after Mass to have a look, and was nearly knocked down by the parson. I began to say something or other, but he ran past me, through from the vicarage, with his coat-tails flying and his man after him. But I stopped the man, and got out of him that Archie was ill, and that the parson was sent for.

"Well, then I went back home and sat down."

The priest drew upon his pipe in silence a moment or two. I felt rather impressed. His airy manner of talking was shot now with a kind of seriousness; and I wondered what was coming next.

He went on almost immediately.

"I heard a bit more as the day wore on. One of my people stayed after Catechism to tell me that the young man was worse, that a doctor had come from Stroud, and another had been wired for from London.

"Well, I waited. I thought I knew what would happen. I thought I had seen a bit more in the old lady than the Dominicans had seen; but what I was going to say to her I knew no more than the dead.

"Then, that night as I was going to bed—I had just said matins and lauds for Michaelmas day—the message came.

"I was halfway upstairs when I heard a knocking at the door, and I went down again and opened it. There was one of the fellows there I had seen on the box of the carriage; and he was out of breath with running. He had a lantern in his hand, because there was a thick mist that night, up from the valley.

"He gave me the lady's compliments, and would I step down? Master Archie was ill. That was all.

"Well, in a minute we were off into the thick of the mist. I took nothing with me but my stole, for it was not a proper sick-call. We said little or nothing to each other. He just told me that Master Archie had been taken ill about ten o'clock, quite suddenly. He didn't know what it was."

The priest paused again for a moment.

Then he went on, almost apologetically.

"You know how it is, gentlemen, when something runs in your head. It may be a tune or a sentence. And I don't know if you've noticed how strong it is sometimes when you have something on your mind.

"Well, what ran in my head was a bit of the Office I

had just said. It was this—I have never forgotten it since—*Stetit Angelus juxta aram templi habens thuribulum aureum in manu sua.*"

He said it again; and then added:

"It comes frequently in the Office, you remember. It was very natural to remember it."

"Well, in half an hour we were at the top of the hill above the house. I think there must have been a moon, because we could see the mist round us like smoke; but nothing of the house, nor even the lights in the top floors below us. It was all white and misty.

"Then we started down through the iron gate and the plantation. I could have lost my way again and again but for the fellow with me; and still we saw nothing of the house till we were close to it on one side; and then I looked up and saw a window like a great yellow door overhead.

"We came round to the front of the house, and there was a carriage there drawn up, with the lamps smoking in the mist, and as we came up I saw that the horses were steaming and blowing. He had just brought the London doctor from Stroud and was waiting for orders, I suppose."

The Canadian paused again.

I was more interested than ever. His descriptions had become queerly particular, and I wondered why. I did not understand yet. The rest too were very quiet.

"We went in through the hall past the stuffed bear that held the calling cards and all that, you know; and then turned in to the left to the big dining room that had been the abbot's chapel. Some fool had left the window open—I suppose they were too flurried to think of it. At any rate, the mist had got in, and made the gas-jets overhead look high up like great stars.

"There was a door open upstairs somewhere, and I could hear whispering.

"Well, we went up the staircase that opened on one side below the gallery that they had put up above the eastern end. The footpace was still there, you know, below the gallery, and the sideboard stood there.

"We came out onto the gallery presently, and my man stopped. Then someone came out with Mrs. Arbuthnot, and the door closed. She saw me standing there and I thought she was going to scream, but the fellow with her in the fur coat—he was the London doctor, I heard afterwards—took her by the arm.

"Well, she was quiet enough then, but as white as death. She had her bonnet on still, just as she must have put it on to go to church with in the morning when the young man was taken ill. She beckoned me along and I went.

"As I was going past the doctor he first shook his head at me and then whispered, as I went on, to keep her quiet. I knew there was no hope then for Archie, and I was sorry, very sorry, gentlemen."

The priest shook his own head meditatively once or twice, leaned forward and spat accurately into the heart of the fire.

"Well, it was a big room that I went into, and, to tell the truth, I left the door open this time, because I was startled by the screen at the bed and all that.

"The screen stood in the corner by the window to keep off the draught, and the bed to one side of it. I could just catch a glimpse of the lad's face on the pillow and the local doctor close by him. There was a woman or two there as well.

"But the worst was that the lad was talking and moaning out loud; but I didn't attend to him then, and, besides, Mrs. Arbuthnot had gone through by another door and I went after her.

"It was a kind of dressing room—Archie's perhaps. There was a tall glass and silver things on the table by the window, and a candle or two burning. She turned round there and faced me, and she looked so deathly that I forgot all about the lad for the present. I just looked out to catch her when she fell. I had seen a woman like that once or twice before.

"Well, she said all that I expected—all about the curse and that, and the sins of the fathers, and it was all her fault for taking the beastly place, and how she would swear to clear out—I couldn't get a word in—and at last she said she'd become a Catholic if the boy lived.

"I did get a word in then, and told her not to talk nonsense. The Church didn't want people like that. They must believe first, and so on—and all the while I was looking out to catch her.

"Well, she didn't hear a word I said, but she sat down all of a sudden, and I sat down too, opposite her, and all the while the boy's voice grew louder and louder from the next room.

"Then she started again, but she hadn't been under way a minute before I had given over attending to her. I was listening to the lad."

The priest stopped again abruptly. His pipe had gone out, but he sucked at it hard and seemed not to notice it. His eyes were oddly alert.

"As I was listening I looked toward the door into the next room. Both that and the one with the gallery over the hall were open, and I saw the mist coming in like smoke.

"I couldn't catch every word the lad said. He was talking in a high droning voice, but I caught enough. It was about a face looking at him through smoke.

"'His eyes are like flames,' he said, 'smoky flames—yellow hair—Are you a priest? … What is that red dress?'—things like that. Well, it seemed pretty tolerable nonsense, and then I—"

Monsignor Maxwell sat up suddenly.

"Good Lord!" he said.

"Yes," drawled the Canadian. "*Stetit Angelus habens thuribulum aureum.*"

He spoke so placidly that I was almost shocked. It seemed astonishing that a man—

Then he went on again:

"Well, I stood up when I heard that, and I faced the old lady.

"'What's the dedication of the chapel,' I said. 'What's the saint? Tell me, woman, tell me!'

"There! I said it like that. Well, she didn't know what I meant, of course, but I got it out of her at last. Of course, it was St. Michael's.

"I sat down then and let her chatter on. I suppose I must have looked a fool, because she took me by the shoulder directly.

"'You aren't listening, Father Jenks,' she said.

"I attended to her then. It seemed as if she wanted me to do something to save him, but I don't think she knew what it was herself, and I'm sure I didn't, not at first at least.

"Then she began again, and all the while the boy was crying out. She wanted to know if her becoming a Catholic would do any good, and to tell the truth I wasn't so sure then myself as I had been before. Then she said she'd give up the house to Catholics, and then at last she said this:

"'Will you take it off, Father? I know you can. Priests can do anything.'

"'Well, I stiffened myself up at that. I was sensible enough not to make a fool of myself, and I said something like this."

He stopped again, sucked vigorously at his cold pipe.

"I said something like this: 'Mind you keep your promise,' I said, 'but as far as I am concerned, I'd let him off.'"

A curious rustle passed round the room, and the priest caught the sound.

"Yes, gentlemen, I said that. I did indeed, and I guess most of you gentlemen would have done the same in my circumstances.

"And this is what happened.

"First the lad's voice stopped, then there was a whispering, then a footstep in the other room, and the next moment Mrs. Arbuthnot was on her feet, with her mouth opened to scream. I had her down again though in time, and, when I turned, a woman was at the door and I could see she had closed the outer door through which the mist came.

"Well, her face told us. The lad had taken the right turn. It was something on the brain, I think, that had dispersed or broken, or something—I forget now—but it seemed to come in pat enough, didn't it, gentlemen?"

The Canadian stopped and leaned back. Was that the end, then?

Father Brent put my question into words.

"And what happened?"

"Well," added the other, drawling more than ever, "Mrs. Arbuthnot did not keep her promise. She's there still, for all I know, and attends the Harvest Festivals as regular as ever. That spoils the story, doesn't it?"

"And the son?" put in the English priest swiftly.

"Well, the son was a bit better. That marriage did not take place. The girl broke it off."

"Well?"

"And Archie's at the English College at this moment studying for the priesthood. I had tea with him at Aragno's yesterday."

VIII

Father Martin's Tale

THE Father Rector announced to us one day at dinner that a friend of his from England had called upon him a day or two before; and that he had asked him to supper that evening.

"There is a story I heard him tell," he said, "some years ago, that I think he would contribute if you cared to ask him, Monsignor. It is remarkable. I remember thinking so."

"Tonight?" said Monsignor.

"Yes, he is coming tonight."

"That will do very well," said the other. "We have no story for tonight."

Father Martin appeared at supper, a grey-haired old man, with a face like a mouse, and large brown eyes that were generally cast down. He had a way at table of holding his hands together with his elbows at his side that bore out the impression of his face.

He looked up deprecatingly and gave a little nervous laugh as Monsignor put his request.

"It is a long time since I have told it, Monsignor," he said.

"That is the more reason for telling it again," said the other priest with his sharp geniality, "or it may be lost to humanity."

"It has met with incredulity," said the old man.

"It will not meet with it here, then," remarked Monsignor. "We have been practising ourselves in the art of believing. Another act of faith will do us no harm."

We explained the circumstances.

Father Martin looked round; and I could see that he was pleased.

"Very well, Monsignor," he said, "I will do my best to make it easy."

When we had reached the room upstairs, the old priest was put into the arm-chair in the centre, drawn back a little so that all might see him; he refused tobacco, propped his chin on his two hands, looking more than ever like a venerable mouse, and began his story. I sat at the end of the semi-circle, near the fire, and watched him as he talked.

"I regret I have not heard the other tales," he said. "It would encourage me in my own. But perhaps it is better so. I have told this so often that I can only tell it in one way, and you must forgive me, gentlemen, if my way is not yours.

"About twenty years ago I had charge of a mission in Lancashire, some fourteen miles from Blackburn, among the hills. The name of the place is Monkswell; it was a little village then, but I think it is a town now. In those days there was only one street, of perhaps a dozen houses on each side. My little church stood at the head of the street, with the presbytery beside it. The house had a garden at the back, with a path running through it to the gate, and beyond the gate was a path leading on to the moor.

"Nearly all the village was Catholic, and had always been so, and I had perhaps a hundred more of my folk scattered about the moor. Their occupation was weaving; that was before the coal was found at Monkswell. Now they have a great church there with a parish of over a thousand.

"Of course, I knew all my people well enough. They are wonderful folk, those Lancashire folk; I could tell you a score of tales of their devotion and faith. There was one woman that I could make nothing of. She lived with her two brothers in a little cottage a couple of miles away from Monkswell, and the three kept themselves by weaving. The two men were fine lads, regular at their religious duties, and at Mass every Sunday. But the woman would not come near the church. I went to her again and again; and before every Easter; but it was of no use. She would not even tell me why she would not come; but I knew the reason. The poor creature had been ruined in Blackburn, and could not hold up her head again. Her brothers took her back, and she had lived with them for ten years, and never once during that time, so far as I knew, had she set foot outside her little place. She could not bear to be seen, you see."

The little pointed face looked very tender and compassionate now, and the brown, beady eyes ran round the circle deprecatingly.

"Well, it was one Sunday in January that Alfred told me that his sister was unwell. It seemed to be nothing serious, he said, and of course he promised to let me know if she should become worse. But I made up my mind that I would go in any case during that week, and see if sickness had softened her at all. Alfred told me too that another brother of his, Patrick, on whom, let it be remembered—" and he held up an admonitory hand—"I had never set eyes, was coming up to them on the next day from London, for a week's holiday. He promised he would bring him to see me later on in the week.

"There was a fall of snow that afternoon, not very deep, and another next day, and I thought I would put off my walk across the hills until it melted, unless I heard that Sarah was worse

"It was on the Wednesday evening about six o'clock that I was sent for.

"I was sitting in my study on the ground floor with the curtains drawn, when I heard the garden gate open and close, and I ran out into the hall, just as the knock came at the back door. I knew that it was unlikely that any should come at that hour, and in such weather, except for a sick-call, and I opened the door almost before the knocking had ended.

"The candle was blown out by the draught, but I knew Alfred's voice at once.

"'She is worse, Father,' he said, 'for God's sake come at once. I think she wishes for the Sacraments. I am going on for the doctor.'

"I knew by his voice that it was serious, though I could not see his face; I could only see his figure against the snow outside. And before I could say more than that I would come at once, he was gone again, and I heard the garden door open and shut. He was gone down to the doctor's house, I knew, a mile further down the valley.

"I shut the hall door without bolting it, and went to the kitchen and told my housekeeper to grease my boots well and set them in my room with my cloak and hat and muffler and my lantern. I told her I had had a sick-call and did not know when I should be back; she had better put the pot on the fire and I would help myself when I came home.

"Then I ran into the church through the sacristy to fetch the holy oils and the Blessed Sacrament.

"When I came back, I noticed that one of the strings of the purse that held the pyx was frayed, and I set it down on the table to knot it properly. Then again I heard the garden gate open and shut."

The priest lifted his eyes and looked round again; there was something odd in his look.

"Gentlemen, we are getting near the point of the story. I will ask you to listen very carefully and to give me your conclusions afterwards. I am relating to you only events, as they happened historically. I give you my word as to their truth."

There was a murmur of assent.

"Well, then," he went on, "at first I supposed it was Alfred come back again for some reason. I put down the string and went to the door without a light. As I reached the threshold there came a knocking.

"I turned the handle and a gust of wind burst in, as it

had done five minutes before. There was a figure standing there, muffled up as the other had been.

"'What is it?' I said. 'I am just coming. Is it you, Alfred?'

"'No, Father,' said a voice—the man was on the steps a yard from me—'I came to say that Sarah was better and does not wish for the Sacraments.'

"Of course I was startled at that.

"'Why, who are you?' I said. 'Are you Patrick?'

"'Yes, Father,' said the man, 'I am Patrick.'

"I cannot describe his voice, but it was not extraordinary in any way; it was a little muffled: I supposed he had a comforter over his mouth. I could not see his face at all. I could not even see if he was stout or thin, the wind blew about his cloak so much.

"As I hesitated, the door from the kitchen behind me was flung open, and I heard a very much frightened voice calling:

"'Who's that, Father?' said Hannah.

"I turned round.

"'It is Patrick Oldroyd,' I said. 'He is come from his sister.'

"I could see the woman standing in the light from the kitchen door; she had her hands out before her as if she were frightened at something.

"'Go out of the draught,' I said.

"She went back at that; but she did not close the door, and I knew she was listening to every word.

"'Come in, Patrick,' I said, turning round again.

"I could see he had moved down a step, and was standing on the gravel now.

"He came up again then, and I stood aside to let him go past me into my study. But he stopped at the door. Still I could not see his face—it was dark in the hall, you remember.

"'No, Father,' he said, 'I cannot wait. I must go after Alfred.'

"I put out my hand toward him, but he slipped past me quickly, and was out again on the gravel before I could speak.

"'Nonsense!' I said. 'She will be none the worse for a doctor; and if you will wait a minute I will come with you.'

"'You are not wanted,' he said rather offensively, I thought. 'I tell you she is better, Father. She will not see you.'

"I was a little angry at that. I was not accustomed to be spoken to in that way.

"'That is very well,' I said, 'but I shall come for all that, and if you do not wish to walk with me, I shall walk alone.'

"He was turning to go, but he faced me again then.

"'Do not come, Father,' he said. 'Come tomorrow. I tell you she will not see you. You know what Sarah is.'

"'I know very well,' I said, 'she is out of grace, and I know what will be the end of her if I do not come. I tell you I am coming, Patrick Oldroyd. So you can do as you please.'

"I shut the door and went back into my room, and as I went, the garden gate opened and shut once more.

"My hands trembled a little as I began to knot the string of the pyx; I supposed then that I had been more angered than I had known"—the old priest looked round again swiftly and dropped his eyes—"but I do not now think that it was only anger. However, you shall hear."

He had moved himself by now to the very edge of his chair where he sat crouched up with his hands together. The listeners were all very quiet.

"I had hardly begun to knot the string before Hannah came in. She bobbed at the door when she saw what I was holding, and then came forward. I could see that she was very much upset by something.

"'Father,' she said, 'for the love of God do not go with that man.'

"'I am ashamed of you, Hannah,' I told her. 'What do you mean?'

"'Father,' she said, 'I am afraid. I do not like that man. There is something the matter.'

"I rose, laid the pyx down and went to my boots without saying anything.

"'Father,' she said again, 'for the love of God do not go. I tell you I was frightened when I heard his knock.'

"Still I said nothing; but put on my boots and went to the table where the pyx lay and the case of oils.

"She came right up to me, and I could see that she was as white as death as she stared at me.

"'I finished putting on my cloak, wrapped the comforter round my neck, put on my hat and took up the lantern.

"'Father,' she said again.

"I looked her full in the face then as she knelt down.

"'Hannah,' I said, 'I am going. Patrick has gone after his brother.'

"'It is not Patrick!' she cried. 'I tell you, Father—"

"Then I shut the door and left her kneeling there.

"It was very dark when I got down the steps; and I hadn't gone a yard along the path before I stepped over my knee into a drift of snow. It had banked up against a gooseberry bush. Well, I saw that I must go carefully; so I stepped back on to the middle of the path, and held my lantern low.

"I could see the marks of the two men plain enough; it was a path that I had made broad on purpose so that I could walk up and down to say my office without thinking much of where I stepped.

"There was one track on this side, and one on that.

"Have you ever noticed, gentlemen, that a man in snow will nearly always go back over his own traces, in preference to anyone else's? Well, that is so—and it was so in this case.

"When I got to the garden gate I saw that Alfred had turned off to the right on his way to the doctor; his marks were quite plain in the light of the lantern, going down the hill. But I was astonished to see that the other man had not gone after him as he said he would; for there was only one pair of footmarks going down the hill; and the other track was plain enough, coming and going. The man must have gone straight home again, I thought.

"Now—"

"One moment, Father Martin," said Monsignor leaning forward; "draw the two lines of tracks here." He put a pencil and paper into the priest's hands.

Father Martin scribbled for a moment or two and then held up the paper so that we could all see it.

As he explained I understood. He had drawn a square for the house, a line for the garden wall, and through the gap ran four lines, marked with arrows. Two ran to the house and two back as far as the gate; at this point one curved sharply round to the right and one straight across the paper beside that which marked the coming.

"I noticed all this," said the old priest emphatically, "because I determined to follow along the double track so far as Sarah Oldroyd's house; and I kept the light turned on to it. I did not wish to slip into a snowdrift.

"Now, I was very much puzzled. I had been thinking it over, of course, ever since the man had gone, and I could not understand it. I must confess that my housekeeper's words had not made it clearer. I knew she did not know Patrick; he had never been home since she had come to me. I was surprised, too, at his behaviour, for I knew from his brother that he was a good Catholic; and—well, you understand, gentlemen—it was very puzzling. But Hannah was Irish, and I knew they had strange fancies sometimes.

"Then, there was something else, which I had better mention before I go any further. Although I had not been frightened when the man came, yet, when Hannah had said that she was frightened, I knew what she meant. It had seemed to me natural that she should be frightened. I can say no more than that."

He threw out his hands deprecatingly, and then folded them again sedately on his hunched knees.

"Well, I set out across the moor, following carefully in the double track of—of the man who called himself Patrick. I could see Alfred's single track a yard to my right; sometimes the tracks crossed.

"I had no time to look about me much, but I saw now and again the slopes to the north, and once when I turned I saw the lights of the village behind me, perhaps a quarter of a mile away. Then I went on again and I wondered as I went.

"I will tell you one thing that crossed my mind, gentlemen. I did wonder whether Hannah had not been right, and if this was Patrick after all. I thought it possible—though I must say I thought it very unlikely—that it might be some enemy of Sarah's—someone she had offended—an infidel, perhaps, but who wished her to die without the Sacraments that she wanted. I thought that; but I never dreamt of—of what I thought afterwards and think now."

He looked round again, clasped his hands more tightly and went on.

"It was very rough going, and as I climbed up at last on to the little shoulder of hill that was the horizon from my house, I stopped to get my breath and turned round again to look behind me.

"I could see my house-lights at the end of the village, and the church beside it, and I wondered that I could see the lights so plainly. Then I understood that Hannah must be in my study and that she had drawn the blind up to watch my lantern going across the snow.

"I am ashamed to tell you, gentlemen, that that cheered me a little; I do not quite know why, but I must confess that I was uncomfortable—I know that I should not have been, carrying what I did, and on such an errand, but I was uneasy. It seemed very lonely out there, and the white sheets of snow made it worse. I do not think that I should have minded the dark so much. There was not much wind and everything was very quiet. I could just hear the stream running down in the valley behind me. The clouds had gone and there was a clear night of stars overhead."

The old priest stopped; his lips worked a little, as I had seen them before, two or three times, during his story. Then he sighed, looked at us and went on.

"Now, gentlemen, I entreat you to believe me. This is what happened next. You remember that this point at which I stopped to take breath was the horizon from my house. Notice that,

"Well, I turned round, and lowered my lantern again to look at the tracks, and a yard in front of me they ceased. They ceased."

He paused again, and there was not a sound from the circle.

"They ceased, gentlemen. I swear it to you, and I cannot describe what I felt. At first I thought it was a mistake; that he had leapt a yard or two—that the snow was frozen. It was not so.

"There a yard to the right were Alfred's tracks, perfectly distinct, with the toes pointing the way from which I had come. There was no confusion, no hard or broken ground, there was just the soft surface of the snow, the trampled path of—of the man's footsteps and mine, and Alfred's a yard or two away."

The old man did not look like a mouse now; his eyes were large and bright, his mouth severe, and his hands hung in the air in a petrified gesture.

"If he had leapt," he said, "he did not alight again."

He passed his hand over his mouth once or twice.

"Well, gentlemen, I confess that I hesitated. I looked back at the lights and then on again at the slopes in front, and then I was ashamed of myself. I did not hesitate long, for any place was better than that. I went on; I dared not run; for I think I should have gone mad if I had lost self-control; but I walked, and not too fast, either; I put my hand on the pyx as it lay on my breast, but I dared not turn my head to right or left. I just stared at Alfred's tracks in front of me and trod in them.

"Well, gentlemen, I did run the last hundred yards; the door of the Oldroyds' cottage was open, and they were looking out for me—and I gave Sarah the last Sacraments, and heard her confession. She died before morning.

"And I have one confession to make myself—I did not go home that night. They were very courteous to me when I told them the story, and made out that they did not wish me to leave their sister; so the doctor and Alfred walked back over the moor together to tell Hannah I should not be back, and that all was well with me.

"There, gentlemen."

"And Patrick?" said a voice.

"Patrick of course had not been out that night."

IX

Mr. Bosanquet's Tale

I think that it was on the second Sunday evening that Father Brent brought in his guest. There was a function of some kind at S. Silvestro—I forget the occasion—a Cardinal had given Benediction and a reception was to follow. At any rate there were only three of us at home, the German, Father Brent and myself.

Of course we talked of our symposium, and the guest, a middle-aged layman, seemed to listen with interest, but he did not say very much. He was a brown-bearded man; he ate slowly and deliberately, and I must confess that I was not particularly impressed with him. Neither did Father Brent try to draw him out. I noticed that he looked at him questioningly once or twice, but he did not actually express his thought till after a little speech from Father Stein.

"But it is a little tiresome to me," said the German, "this talk of footsteps and voices and visions. If that world in which we believe is spiritual, as we know it is, how is it that it presents itself to us under material images? These things are but appearances, but what is the reality?"

Father Brent turned to his friend.

"Well?" he said. "What now?"

Mr. Bosanquet smiled and became grave again over his pastry.

"You will repeat it then?" persisted the priest.

The Englishman looked up for an instant, and I met his grave eyes.

"If these gentlemen really wish it," he said briefly.

Father Brent sighed with satisfaction.

"That is excellent," he said.

Then he explained.

Mr. Bosanquet had a story, it seemed, but had entirely refused to relate it to a mixed company. He had had a certain experience once which had changed his life and it was not an experience to be described at random. There was no ghost in it, it was wholly unsensational, but it had, Father Brent thought, a peculiar interest of its own. He had persuaded his friend to sup with us, knowing that we should be but few, and hoping that the atmosphere might be found favourable. This was the gist of what he was saying, but he was interrupted by the entrance of Beppo with the coffee.

"Shall we have coffee upstairs?" he said.

Then we rose and went upstairs.

It was a few minutes before we settled down, and Mr. Bosanquet seemed in no hurry to begin. But a silence fell presently, and finally the young priest leaned forward.

"Now, Bosanquet," he said.

Mr. Bosanquet set his cup down, crossed his legs and began. He spoke in a very quiet, unemotional voice.

"My friend has told you that this experience of mine is unsensational. In a manner of speaking he is right. It is unsensational, since it deals with nothing other than that which we must all go through sooner or later; but I think it has a certain interest from the fact that it is an experience of which, except under very peculiar circumstances, none of us will ever be able to give an account. It concerns the act of dying."

He paused for a moment.

"Yes, the act of dying," he repeated, "for I firmly believe that that is precisely what I did. I passed the point on which death is dogmatically declared by the doctors to have taken place. I underwent, that is, what is called 'legal death,' but I did not of course reach that further state called 'somatic death.'"

Father Brent voiced my question.

"Please explain," he said.

"Oh—well. The body, as we know, consists of cells; but there is a certain unity, usually identified with the vital principle, which merges these into one entity—so that if one member suffer all the members suffer with it. Legal death is when this vital principle leaves the body. The lungs cease to act; the heart is motionless. But when this has taken place there yet remains a further stage. The cells, for a certain period, have a kind of life of their own. There is no vital union between them; the nerve system is suspended; and somatic death, marked by the *rigor mortis*, the stiffening of the cells, indicates the moment when the cells too, even individually, cease to live. But the man is dead, doctors tell us, sometimes many hours before *rigor mortis* sets in. In fact, in the case of some of the saints, *rigor mortis* appears never to have set in at all; their limbs, we are told, retain softness and elasticity. There is no corruption, at least in the ordinary sense."

Father Stein grunted and nodded.

"In my case," pursued the Englishman, "I was declared dead, and, as I learned afterwards, remained in that state about half an hour. It was after my body had been washed and the face bound up, that I returned to life."

I sat up in my chair at that. At least he was explicit enough. He glanced at me.

I can show you my death certificate, if you care to come to my hotel tomorrow," he said. "I obtained it from the doctor—cancelled however, you understand.

"Well—this is what took place.

"The cause of death was exhaustion, following upon *angina pectoris* with other complications. I will spare you the details, and begin at once at the point at which I was declared to be dying. Up to that point I had suffered extraordinary agony, tempered by morphia. I did not know that such pain was possible.... At the moments of the spasms, before each injection took effect, it seemed to me that I did not suffer pain, so much as become pain. There was no room for anything else but pain. Then there came the beginning of the dulness of it; it retired and stood off from me. I was still conscious of it, as of a storm passing away, till all sank into a kind of peace. Then, after a long while as it seemed, the dulness lifted, and I came up again to the surface, becoming aware of the world, though of course this bore a certain aspect of unreality, owing to the effects of the drug.

"Well, I said I would leave all that out.

"The last time I came up, I knew I was dying. It was all quite different. Things no longer bore that close relation to me that they had had before. I opened my eyes just enough to let me see my hands lying out on the counterpane, and the hillock of my feet, and even the lower part of the brass supports at the end of my bed; but I could not raise my eyelids higher, and almost immediately I closed them again.

"The sense of touch too was changed. Once or twice when I have been falling asleep in my chair I have noticed the same phenomenon. I could not tell by feeling—unless I moved them—whether my fingers rested on the counterpane or not. I did move them then, with that curious clawing motion that dying people use, simply in order to realize my relations with material surroundings. That of course, as I know now, is the reason of those motions. It is not an involuntary contraction of the muscles; it is the will trying to get back into touch with the world.

"But the sense of hearing, oddly enough, was almost preternaturally acute. Others undergoing anaesthetics have told me the same. It is the last sense to leave them, and the first to return. I could hear a continual minute series of sounds—not at all painfully loud, but absolutely distinct. There was my sister's breathing, irregular and uneven beside me. I knew by it that she was trying not to break down. I could hear four timepieces ticking—her watch and the doctor's, and that of the travelling clock over the fire, and the Dutch clock in the hall below. Then there were the country sounds in the distance, and the breeze in the creepers outside my window.

"With regard to taste and smell—they were there—a kind of sour sweetness, if I may say so—but they did not interest me; they were below my level, if I may express it like that.

"Well, I said just now that I knew I was dying. It was as if through all my being there was a steady, smooth retirement from the world. I was perfectly able to reflect—in fact I reflected as I have never been able before or since. Do you know the sensation of coming down from town and sitting out in the darkness after dinner in the garden? The silence, after the clatter and glare of London makes it possible, seems to let the mind free. One is both alert and reflective—both at once. One's thoughts are the immediate object of one's contemplation. It was rather like that, only far more pronounced. And in that freedom from the presence of matter I realized perfectly what was happening.

"Now I must tell you at once that I was not at all frightened. My religion seemed to stand off from me with the rest of the world. I had been, up to that time, what may be called a 'conventional believer.' I had never doubted exactly—for I always realized that it was absurd for me to criticize what was so obviously the highest standard of morality and faith—I mean Christianity. But neither was I particularly interested. I had lived like other people. I attended church, I repeated my prayers, and I had conventional views of heaven, with which was mixed up a good deal of agnosticism. In a word, I think I may say that I had Hope, but not Faith—not Faith, that is, as you Catholics seem to have it."

This was the first hint I had had that Mr. Bosanquet was not a Catholic, and I glanced up at Father Brent. He too glanced at me in a half-warning, half-suggestive look. I understood.

"I was not frightened, then," continued the other tranquilly. "My religion, as I see now, was altogether bound up with the world. Even my thoughts went no further than images. I conceived of heaven as in a picture, of our Lord as a superhuman man, of death as of a swift passage through the air. We are all bound, of course, by our limitations to do that; but I had not realized the inadequacy of such images. I conceived of Eternity and spiritual existence in terms of time and space, and I had not really even as much faith as that of the agnostic who recognizes that these are inadequate, and therefore foolishly believes that the reality is unknowable—though in one sense indeed it is."

Once more the German priest murmured; and I saw now why this man had been encouraged to tell his story.

"Well, then," he continued, "when the world retired from me with the approach of death, my religion retired naturally with it. (That seems to me so obvious now!) and I was left, moving swiftly *inwards*, if I may express it so, towards a state of which I was completely ignorant. I was dying, as I suppose animals die. I never lost self-consciousness for a moment. As a rule, of course, one realizes self-consciousness, as philosophers tell us, by self-differentiation from what is not self. The baby learns it gradually by touching and looking. The dying lose it by ceasing to touch and see—or, rather, they lose that mode of realizing it, and enter into themselves instead. It is a transcendent kind of self-consciousness—different altogether.

"I had then a vague kind of anxiety, but I was perfectly peaceful. I had no particular remembrance of sins, no faith or love or hope—nothing but a sense of extreme *naturalness*, if I may express it so. It seemed as if I had known all this all along—as a stone thrown into the air would, if it had consciousness, realize the inevitability of its curve as it neared the earth. I was to die—well, that was the corollary of having lived!

"Well, this inevitable movement inwards went on, as it seemed to me, very swiftly. Each instant that I applied my consciousness it seemed to me as if I had gone a great way since the previous instant; the only thing that astonished me was the distance there was to travel. It was a sensation—how shall I express it?—a sensation of sinking swiftly into an inner depth of which I had not guessed the extent. I wondered, in a complacent, half-curious kind of way, as to what exactly would be the end—how things would be visualized when I passed finally from the body—and, such things as I pictured, I pictured of course in terms of time and space. I—I thought—my essential self, whatever that was, would at a certain moment pass a certain line, and emerge on the other side; and there things would be rather as they had been on earth, thinner…spiritual—I should see faces, perhaps, forms, places, all in a kind of delicate light. What really happened was a complete surprise."

Mr. Bosanquet paused, and in a meditative kind of way winked several times at the fire. He showed no emotion. He seemed to me merely to be recalling the best phrases to use.

"Well," he said, "I have told this story before, and each time before telling it I have thought that I had got the point and could really describe what happened, and each time I have been disappointed…. Of course it must be so.

There are simply no words or illustrations. I must do the best I can.

"Well, this process went on, and after a while I perceived plainly that my senses were fading. I believe I opened my eyes; so I was told afterwards—opened them wide; but at any rate I saw nothing this time except blurred lines and colours, rather like the reverse side of a carpet. They were rather bewildering; but they soon went, leaving nothing but a streaked greyness that darkened rapidly.

"I could no longer move my hands—or in fact recall to myself by feeling, any material thing at all. I seemed to have lost relations with my body. Neither could I move my lips or tongue—taste had gone—I don't think I had ever understood before how taste depends on the will and on the movement of the tongue—much more so than any of the other senses which are more or less passive.

"And then quite suddenly I perceived that hearing had ceased also. There had been no drumming in my ears, as I had half expected; I think there had been at some time previously a clear singing of one high note which had rather bothered me; and I suppose that it was then that hearing had gone, but I did not notice it till I thought about it.

"And then there was one more thing more strange than all… I began to perceive that my will was not myself.

"Most of us are accustomed to think that it is. It is so closely united with that which is the very self that we usually identify them. Sometimes we are even more foolish, and identify our emotion with ourselves, and think that our moods are our character. The fact is, of course, that the intellect is the most superficial of our faculties; there are simply scores of things that we cannot understand in the least, but of which for all that we are as certain as of our own existence. Next to that comes the emotion; it is certainly nearer to us than intellect, though not much, and thirdly comes the will.

"Now the will is quite close to us; it is that through which we consciously act, after having heard the reasons for or against action suggested by the other faculties. But the will is, after all, a faculty of itself—not self itself.

"I began to see this from the way it was labouring, like an exhausted engine; it still throbbed and moved; it turned this way and that, directing the all but dead faculties outside to move in this or that direction—to think and to perceive. But I began to see clearly now that the real self was something altogether apart—existing simply in another mode. There—that is the point—*in another mode.*

"Now, in this matter I feel hopeless. I simply cannot express what I knew, and know, to be the central fact of our existence. I can say no more than that Self, that which lies far behind everything else, exists in as different a mode from all else, as—as the inner meaning of a phrase of music is apart from the existence of a dog walking up the street. There is simply no common term which can be applied to them both.

"Well, I perceived my will to be labouring, very slowly and clumsily; and I perceived that it would not be able to move much longer. (You must understand that this 'perceiving', as I call it, was not the act of my intellect; it was simply a deep intuitive knowledge dwelling in that which I call Self.)

"Then I suddenly became aware that it was important for my will to fall in the right direction: I understood that this would make well the whole difference to me.... I knew that this would be my last conscious act.

"You ask me how I knew what was the right direction. Well—I must go slowly here."

He paused for a moment, then he went on very slowly, picking his words.

"I began, I think I may say, to be clearly and vividly conscious of two *centres*; there was Self, and there was Another. This Other was at present completely hidden from me. I was only aware of it as one may be aware of the presence of a huge personality behind an impenetrable curtain. But I perceived that this Other was the only important thing.

"Well...my will was reeling; there was no discomfort, no fear, or pain, or anxiety, and I—whatever that is—watched it, as a man may watch a top in its last swift twistings on its side. I had still some control over it; I knew that it was my will, it still was linked to me in a way.... Then I put out my energy (remember, there was no conscious perception of anything—nothing but a perfectly unreflective instinct) and tried to wrench that rolling thing round to a position of rest—ah, how shall I put it—a position of rest pointing towards this other centre.

"And, as I made that effort I lost touch with it—I have no idea whether I succeeded—and at the same instant, if I may call it so, something happened."

Mr. Bosanquet leaned back and sighed.

"Every word is wrong," he said. "You understand that, do you not?"

I nodded two or three times. I kept my eyes on his face. He glanced round at the other two. Then he went on, shifting his attitude a little:

"Well, this something… I suppose I could give half a dozen illustrations, but none of them would be adequate. Let me give you two or three.

"When a man falls in love suddenly, his whole centre changes. Up to that point he has, probably, referred everything to himself—considered things from his own point. When he falls in love the whole thing is shifted; he becomes a part of the circumference—perhaps even the whole circumference; someone else becomes the centre. For example, things he hears and sees are referred in future instantly to this other person; he ceases to be acquisitive, his entire life, if it is really love, is pulled sideways; he does not desire to get, but to give. That is why it is the noblest thing in the world.

"Secondly, imagine that you had lived all your life in a certain house, and had got to know every detail of it perfectly; you had walked about in the garden, too, and looked through the railings, and thought you knew pretty fairly what the country was like. Then, one morning, after you had got up and dressed, you went to your bedroom door, opened it and went out; and that very instant found yourself not in the passage, but on the top of a high mountain with a strange country visible for miles all round, and no house or human being near you.

"Thirdly (and this perhaps is the best illustration after all), imagine that you were looking at a picture, and had become absorbed in it; and then, without any warning at all the picture suddenly became a chord of music which you heard, and which you recognized to be identical with the picture—not merely analogous to it—but the actual picture translated, transubstantiated and trans-accidentated into sound.

"Now, those are the three illustrations I generally use in telling this story; there are others, but I think these are the best.

"Well, it was like that; but you must please to remember that these are only like charcoal sketches of something which is colour rather than shape. But, briefly, these are the nearest similitudes I can think of.

"First, although I remained the same, I became aware that I simply was not the centre of what I experienced. It was not I who primarily existed at all. There was Something—I call it Something, because the word Person simply bears no resemblance to the Personality of this other existence, at least, no more than a resemblance; because this other Personality was as different from, and as far above, our own as the personality of a philosopher is different from the corresponding thing in a pebble. I became aware (at least this was what I told myself afterwards), I became aware of real Existence for the first time in my experience. I myself then, became merely a speck in a circumference. Yet—and this is why I spoke of love—I also became aware that while I had not lost my individuality, yet this other Being was the only thing that mattered at all, and, further—well, I may as well say it outright, that in the very depth of this Existence was Human Nature—yes,

Human Nature. I knew it instantly. I never before had had
the faintest idea of what the Incarnation really meant.

"Secondly, the whole of everything was different—as
startlingly different as the change of my second illustra-
tion. I had expected to find a kind of continuation. There
was, in one sense, no continuation at all—nothing in the
least like what experience had led me to expect. It was
completely abrupt.

"Thirdly, in another sense, what I found was not only
the consequence of what had preceded—it was not simply
the result; but it was identical with what had preceded. It
was the picture becoming sound—the essence of my pre-
vious life was here in other terms. It simply was. The whole
thing was complete. You may call this Judgment; well, that
will do; but it was a Judgment in which there was no ques-
tion of concurrence or protest. It was inevitably true.

"Let me take even one more illustration.

"Once I went with my brother into a glasshouse in
autumn. He smelt a certain flower, and then, rather excit-
edly, asked me to smell it. I shut my eyes and smelt it. Prac-
tically instantly the whole thing became sound and sight.
I saw the terrace at home in summer, and heard the bees.
I looked up.

"'Well?' he said.

"'The terrace in summer,' I said.

"'Exactly.'

"Well, it was like that. There was no question about it.

"Now, I have taken some time to tell this; but I must
make it clear that there was absolutely no time in the expe-
rience, no sense of progression. It was not merely that I

was absorbed, but that time had no existence. This is how I know it.

"Simultaneously with all this I heard one noise; and immediately time began I began to consider. Presently I heard another noise, then another, like a great drum being beaten. Then the noises went; and there was absolute silence, of which I was aware, and others came in, a rustling, a footstep, the sound of words. I was entirely absorbed in these. I heard the sound of water, a door opening, the ticking of a clock. I was conscious of no consideration about these things, and no sensation of any kind; it was as if my brain had become one ear which heard. This went on—well, I may say it was ten seconds or ten years. Time meant nothing to me. I only know even now that it existed because one thing followed another. I did not reflect at all.

"At last, after this had gone on, it was as if a new note had struck. Another sense began to move—the sense of sight. I first became aware of darkness, then came a glimmer, with a sensation of flickering. Then touch. I became aware of a constraint somewhere in the universe; it was a long time before I knew that I myself was feeling it. I did not perceive sensation: I was it.

"Well—these waxed and waxed; then my will stirred; and I became aware that I could choose, that I could acquiesce or resent—then emotion; and I found myself disliking certain sensations. Then I began to wonder and question again, and ask myself why and what—"

Mr Bosanquet broke off abruptly.

"Well, I needn't go on. To put it in a word I was coming

back to ordinary life. Half an hour after the doctor had said that I was dead, and about three minutes after the nurse had finished with me, just as she was looking at me, in fact, before going out of the room, I made a sound with my lips. The rest happened as you would expect: there was nothing interesting in that.

"'But this is the point I want to make clear. Those noises I heard like a drum, followed by the silence, were, without doubt, the sounds my own body made in dying.

"It was at that point that I died; and the next sounds that I began to hear were the noise the nurse made in washing me and laying me out. There is no question about that. I asked about all the details, minutely.

"But the thing that seemed to me so strange at first was the fact that I had died 'before' that, as we say. That complete change of the mode of existence undoubtedly marked death; and the particular instant of death must have been that at which I became aware of the change, and of the severance of my will from myself.

"But I understood it presently. The explanation, I think, must be this:

"There is always a certain space of time between an incident happening and our perception of it—infinitesimally small if we are observing it; but yet it is there. Well, when I made that final effort of will, I died; but dying had begun before that. I had only regarded dying from the purely internal side; it took, in my soul, the form of severance from my will. At that same instant, since we must speak in terms of time, I was in the spiritual mode of existence, where there is simply no time, but which includes all time and all one's previous experience, and in practically the same 'instant' I was back again, and experiencing the physical phenomena of dying. The drum-note was either my throat or heart, I suppose—the silence that followed was the body's perception of death, worked out in terms of time.

"We may say then this, impossible as it sounds, that death had taken place at a given moment in time—that that inner real self, behind the will, which I have spoken of, simultaneously experienced severance from the body, and was, immediately in our own mode of existence, which, although reckoned as time was an instant, was in fact simply eternity with its inevitable consequences. But, after eternity had been experienced, since I suppose again I must say, 'after'—it ceased to be experienced; and all this was enacted in time. Then—"

Mr. Bosanquet sat up, smiling suddenly.

"It is useless—I am boring you."

I roused myself to answer with an energy I had not expected.

"No—please—"

"Well, in one sentence.... Then I died."

He leaned back with an air of finality.

"But—but one question," I protested. "You spoke of Judgment. Was the result happiness or unhappiness?"

He shook his head, smiling.

X

Father Maddox's Tale

"This is a most disappointing story," began old Father Maddox, with a deprecating smile. "You will find it as annoying as the 'Lady and the Tiger'; there is no answer. Or rather there are two, and you may take your choice, and no one can contradict you or satisfy you that you are right." There was a moment's pause as the priest elaborately placed a pinch of brown powder on his thumb-nail and inhaled it noisily through first one nostril and then the other, with an indescribable grimace. He flicked the specks away, wiped his nose with a magenta cotton hand-kerchief, replaced his snuff-box, folded his hands, cocked one knee over the other, and proceeded. Father Maddox had looked so profound just now that Canon Maxwell had turned and challenged him; and here was the result. As he talked I watched his large, flat foot, creased across the toes, as if an extra two inches had been added subsequently. Its size and shape seemed the very embodiment of common sense.

"About fourteen or fifteen years ago," he began, "I was at a mission in the Fens—quite a little place—you would not know its name—about ten miles from Ely. I was very much pleased to hear one day that an old friend of mine had taken a house about seven miles away at a place called Baddenham—because, you know, the life of a priest at such a mission is apt to be very lonely, and I looked forward to his company now and again. The neighbouring Protestant clergy would have nothing to say to me."

The old man smiled at the company in his deprecating manner and went on:

"About a week later my friend, Mr. Hudson—a bachelor, by the way, and a Fellow of one of the Cambridge colleges, and a great recluse—my friend wrote and asked me to spend a Monday to Wednesday with him. There was a novelist coming to stay with him—I think I had better not mention his name; we will call him Mr. Baxter—and this—er—Mr. Baxter wished to meet a Catholic priest for a particular reason that you shall hear presently. I was very much pleased at this, for I had often heard the writer's name, as all of you have, Reverend Fathers"—he smiled slyly—"and I liked his books. He was always very kind to us poor Papists, though I believe he was a man of no religion himself.

"Well, I gave out that there would be no Mass on Tuesday or Wednesday—and I said, too, where I was going, in case there was a sick-call, though that was not likely; and on the Monday afternoon I walked up with my bag from Baddenham station to the Hall.

"It was a very fine old house, very old—built, I suppose, about the beginning of the sixteenth century—and it stood in the middle of a little park of about a hundred acres. It was L-shaped, of red brick, with a little turret at the north end, and had a little walled garden on the south.

"Mr. Baxter was not come yet; he would be there for dinner, my friend told me; and, sure enough, about half-past seven he came.

"He was a little man—not at all what I expected—with black hair a little grey at the temples, clean-shaven, with spectacles. He was a very quick man—I could see that. He talked a great deal at dinner; and it seemed, from what my friend said, that he was come down there from town to make a beginning at his new book, which was to be on the days of Elizabeth."

Father Maddox stopped, and looked round smiling.

"No, gentlemen, you cannot guess from that. The book was never written, as you shall hear."

There was a murmur of disappointment, and Father Brent, who had sat forward suddenly, sank back again, smiling too.

"Well, it seemed that Mr. Baxter wished to meet a priest, because he was anxious to hear a little of how Catholics managed in those days, what it was that priests carried with them on their travels, and so forth; but it appeared presently that Catholics were not to be the principal characters of the story, though he thought of bringing them in.

"'I must have a priest, Father Maddox,' he said. 'There might be some good side-scenes made out of that. Please tell me everything you can.'

"Well, I told him all I could, and about the missal and altar-stone at Oscott, and so on; and I told him, too, the kind of work that priests had to do, and their dangers, and the martyrdoms.

"'Did many give in?' he asked.

"'Apostatize?' I said. 'Oh, a few—very few.'

"He seemed very thoughtful at that, and after we had smoked a little he asked if we might go round the house.

He liked to know what sort of a place he was sleeping in, he said. He seemed to get very much excited with the house: it was certainly an interesting old place, with several panelled rooms, uneven floors, diamond-paned windows, and all the rest. There was a curious little place, too, in the turret: a kind of watchtower, it seemed, with tiny windows, or rather spy-holes, all round. I never remember having seen anything like it elsewhere; and it was approached by an oaken stair from the room below. It was so small that two people could hardly turn round in it together.

"Well, we saw everything, going with candles, and came down again at last to the old parlour, and there we sat till nearly midnight, Mr. Baxter asking me all sorts of questions, many of which I could not answer.

"When our host took up his candle to go to bed, Mr. Baxter said he would sit up a bit, so we left him and went upstairs.

"I am always a poor sleeper, particularly in a new house, and I tossed about a long time. It was winter, by the way— or rather, late autumn—so I had a fire in my room, which was at the top of the stairs, the first door on the right.

"Then, when I did go to sleep at last, I dreamed that I was still awake. I don't know whether anyone else has ever had that; but I often do. I remember what I dreamed, too. It was that I was back again in the parlour with the other two, and that I was trying to sleep in my chair, but that Mr. Baxter would not be quiet; he kept walking up and down the room, waving his hands and talking to himself, and that the other man—ah, wait!"

The priest paused.

"I have not explained properly. At first, in my dream, the third man was certainly Mr. Hudson—at least, I supposed so—but after a while it seemed not to be; it was someone else, I did not know who, and I could not remember his face. This third man, apparently, was not trying to sleep; he was standing in the corner of the room, in the shadow, watching Mr. Baxter as he went up and down. Well, this went on a long while, and then at last I awoke, wide awake, and lay much annoyed. I was hardly fully awake before I heard Mr. Baxter come upstairs. I heard his bedroom candle clink as he lit it in the hall below, and then I heard the creak of one of his shoes, which I had noticed before. He came upstairs, past my door, walking rather quickly as his way was; and I heard him shut the door of his room, which was at the further end of the landing. Then I went to sleep."

Father Maddox paused, took another pinch of snuff, looking round on us.

"Is that all clear, so far?" he asked.

There was a murmur of assent, and he went on:

"Well, Mr. Baxter was very late at breakfast. He did not come down till we had finished, and I thought he looked very tired. He was plainly rather excited, too, and as he helped himself at the sideboard he turned round.

"'My dear Hudson,' he said, 'what a house this is of yours! It has really inspired me. I sat up till nearly three, and I believe I have got a first-rate idea.'

"Of course we asked what it was, and as he ate his porridge he told us.

"He was going to bring in an apostate priest—a man, sincere enough in his faith, who gave way under torture.

He was to be the son of a family who remained good Catholics, and he was to come home again to the very place where he had been caught, and where his mother was still living. It would be a good situation, thought Mr. Baxter—the apostate son, believing all the time, and his mother, who of course loved him, but who hated the thought of what he had done—and these two should live together in the house where they had said good-bye two months before, when the mother thought her son was going to his martyrdom. It seemed to me quite possible, and I said so; and that pleased Mr. Baxter very much.

"'Yes,' he said. 'And, Hudson, would you mind if I took this house as the scene of it? It seems to me just made for it. That little turret room, you know, would be the place from which the priest saw the constables surrounding the house, and the room underneath could be the chapel. And think what he would think when he saw them again! Do you mind?'

"Mr. Hudson, of course, said that he would be highly honoured, and all the rest; and so it was settled.

"Presently Mr. Baxter was off again.

"'It is quite extraordinary,' he said, 'how vivid the whole thing is to me—the character of the priest, his little ways, the weakness in his face, and all the rest; and the mother too, a fine silent old lady, intensely religious and intensely fond of her son, and knowing that he had only yielded through pain. He would limp a little, from the rack, and not be able to manage his knife very well.'

"I asked him presently how he worked out his characters—and how far—before he began to write.

"'Generally,' he said, 'I leave a good deal to the time of writing. I first get the idea, and perhaps the general appearance of each person, and of course the plot; then I begin to write; and after about a chapter or two the people seem to come alive and to do it all themselves, and I only have to write it down as well as I can. I think most writers find it happens like that. But this time I must say it is rather different: I don't think I have ever had anything so vivid before. I am beginning to think that my Catholics will have to be the principal people after all. At any rate, I shall begin with them.

"He talked like this a good deal at breakfast, and seemed quite excited. It all seemed to me very odd, and particularly so when he said that, when he was once in the middle of the book, his characters seemed almost more real than living people; it was a kind of trance, he said; the real world became shadowy, and the world of imagination the real one. Since then I have asked one or two other writers, and they have told me the same.

"Well, when we met at lunch I began to understand how true it all was. He was actually in a kind of waking dream; he had been writing hard all the morning, and it seemed as if he could pay no attention to anything. He didn't talk much—hardly a word, in fact—and finally Mr. Hudson said something about it.

"'My dear man,' said the other, 'I really can't attend. I am very sorry; but it's a kind of obsession now. I tell you that this book is the only thing that matters to me in the least. They are all waiting for me now in the study—Mr. Jennifer the apostate, his mother, and an old manservant of the house. I can't possibly come out this afternoon; this chapter has got to get done.'

"He really was quite pale with excitement, and he rushed out again as soon as he had finished.

"Well, Mr. Hudson and I went out together, and we got back about four, just as the evening was beginning to close in. We had tea alone; Mr. Baxter had ordered it for himself, it seemed, when our host went in to see if he was coming.

"'He is working like a madman,' he said, when he came back. 'I have just given him the keys of the turret; he says he is going up there before it is quite dark to see how far away the priest could have seen the constables round the house.'

"After tea I went upstairs to put on my cassock and change my shoes, and as I went into my room I heard the study door open and Mr. Baxter come out. I watched him, from inside, go past, and heard him cross the landing to get to the turret room and the stairs.

"Now I must explain."

Father Maddox paused; then he leaned forward, drew up the little table by his side, and began to arrange books in the shape of an L.

"This is the first floor, you understand. This small book stands for the horizontal of the L. My room was here, in the angle, at the top of the stairs. Mr. Baxter's room was on the right, past mine, at the end of the horizontal. Just opposite his room was the one which he said was to be the chapel, and out of this room rose the turret-stairs. This part of the house is only two stories high, but the turret itself is high enough to see over the roofs of the upright part of the L, as those rooms, although there are three stories of them, are much lower than these others.

"Very well, then…. I heard Mr. Baxter go across and go into the chapel room. Then I heard his footsteps stop; he was looking, he told us afterwards, at the place where the altar would have stood, and so on.

"When I had changed my things I thought I would go out and see how he was getting on. It was very nearly dark by now, so I took one of my candles and went across. The door of the chapel room was open and I went in."

Father Maddox paused once more. I could see that a climax was coming, and I must confess that I felt oddly excited. He seemed such a common-sense man, too.

"Now, those of you who have ever shot over dogs know what happens when a dog points; how he stiffens all over and is all strung up tight. Well, that is what Mr. Baxter was doing. He was standing, rather crouching, with his hands out on either side, palms down, staring sideways up the little staircase that led to the turret. This staircase, I must tell you, ran diagonally up across the further end of the room, like a loft staircase. There were no open bannisters; it was masked by panelling, and was generally closed by a door in the panelling; but this was open now, and, as I said, he had twisted his head sideways so that his eyes looked up it—up to the right.

✳ "Well, at first I thought he was calculating something, but he did not move as I came in; he was like a statue. I said something, but he paid no attention. I went right up to him.

"'Mr. Baxter,' I said, 'I have come to see—'

"Then a sort of horrid moan came from him, and he suddenly jumped back and seized me by the arm so that the candle dropped and we were almost in the dark; but I caught a sight of his face.

"'He is coming down, he is coming down, Father,' he whispered. 'Oh, for God's sake!' Then he gave a great wrench at my arm, still moaning; and somehow we were out of the room, across the landing, and half tumbling downstairs together. Mr. Hudson ran out at the noise, and somehow we got him into the study and in a deep chair, and he went off into a swoon."

The old man paused, and looked round with rather a tremulous smile; and, I must confess, the silence in the room was very much marked.

"Well, half an hour later Mr. Baxter seemed himself again. He was able to tell us what had happened. It seemed that he had gone into the room, and, as I had thought, had stopped a moment or two there, trying to imagine the old arrangements that he had invented—*invented*, Reverend Fathers; remember that: there was no tradition about the house at all. Neither then nor afterwards. Then he had gone to the staircase to go up to the turret.

"Now, this is what he said he saw—he told us all this gradually, of course. He saw a man in a cassock and cap standing on the top step of the little stairs, looking out through the tiny window that is in the wall opposite. At first he thought it was I. It was very dark; there was only a little dim light from the turret room behind the figure, and his face, as I said, was pressed against the darkening window, exactly as if he were watching for somebody. He had called out, and the figure had turned, and he had seen it to be a young man, under thirty, with very large dark eyes, thin lips, and a little round chin. He had seen that absolutely plainly in the light from the window. He also saw, as he looked, that the face was exactly that of the priest whom he had imagined in his story, and who, as he had told us at lunch, was completely vivid to his brain. Well, he had simply stared and stared. He said that fear was not the word at all: it was a kind of paralysis. He could not move or take his eyes away; and what was odd too was that this other man seemed paralysed too. He said that the lips moved, and that the eyes were wide and dilated, but that he said nothing. Mr. Baxter had heard me come in, and at the sound the figure at the top of the stairs had winced and clasped its hands, and that then, with some sort of hopeless gesture, it had begun to come down. Then I had spoken, and Mr. Baxter had turned and seized my arm.

"Well, there was no doing anything with Mr. Baxter. He lay still, starting at every sound, telling us this little by little. Then he asked that his things might be packed. He must go away at once, he said.

"We told him what nonsense it all was, and how he had been worked up; and Mr. Hudson talked about the artistic temperament and all the rest. But it was no good; he must go; and Mr. Hudson rang the bell to give the order. As Mr. Baxter stood up at last, still all white and trembling, he saw his manuscript on the table, and before I could say a word he had seized it and tossed it into the fire: there would be thirty or forty pages, I should think.

"We went to the door to see him off—he had entirely refused to go upstairs again; even his boots were brought down—and he hardly said anything more after he had told us his story; he said he would write in a day or two. Then we went back to the parlour and talked it all over.

"Of course we said what we thought. It seemed to us plain enough that he had worked himself up to a most frightful pitch of nerves, and—well, all the rest of it. The whole thing, we said, was sheer imagination; you see, it was not that there was any story about the house.

"Just as Mr. Hudson was going to dress, the butler came in."

Father Maddox stopped again.

"Now, Reverend Fathers, this is the point of the story, and you may draw your own conclusions. The butler came in, looking rather puzzled, and asked how many there would be for dinner. Mr. Hudson told him two: Mr. Baxter was not coming back.

"'I beg your pardon, sir,' said the man; 'but what of the other gentleman?'

"'Why, here he is,' said my friend. 'One and one makes two, Manthorpe.'

"'But the gentleman upstairs, sir, and his servant?'

"'You may imagine we jumped rather at that; and he told us then.

"One of the maids going across the landing ten minutes before had seen two persons—one of them a young gentleman, she said, in a long cloak, and the other an old man, his servant, she thought, for he was carrying a great bag—come out of Mr. Baxter's room and go into the turret room. *The young gentleman was limping*, she said. 'She had particularly noticed that.'"

Father Maddox stopped, and there was a sudden chorus of questions.

"No," he said, "there was no explanation at all. The maid had not been at all frightened; she had supposed it was another visitor come by the same train as that by which Mr. Baxter had come the night before. She had not followed them; she had just gone and told Manthorpe, and asked where the gentleman was to sleep. We went everywhere—into the turret room, up the stairs—everywhere. There was nothing; there never was anything; none at all.

"Now you see the difficulty, Reverend Fathers," ended the old man, smiling again. "The question is, did Mr. Baxter's imagination in a kind of way create those things so strongly that not only he saw them, but the maid as well—a kind of violent thought transference? Or was it that there was truth in the story—that something of the sort had happened in the house, and that this was the reason why, firstly, the idea had come so vividly to Mr. Baxter's mind, and secondly that he and the maid had actually seen—well, what they did see?"

He took out his snuff-box.

XI

Father Macclesfield's Tale

MONSIGNOR Maxwell announced next day at dinner that he had already arranged for the evening's entertainment. A priest, whose acquaintance he had made on the Palatine, was leaving for England the next morning; and it was our only chance therefore of hearing his story. That he had a story had come to the Canon's knowledge in the course of a conversation on the previous afternoon.

"He told me the outline of it," he said, "I think it very remarkable. But I had a great deal of difficulty in persuading him to repeat it to the company this evening. But he promised at last. I trust, gentlemen, you do not think I have presumed in begging him to do so."

Father Macclesfield arrived at supper. He was a little unimposing dry man, with a hooked nose and grey hair. He was rather silent at supper; but there was no trace of shyness in his manner as he took his seat upstairs, and without glancing round once, began in an even and dispassionate voice:

"I once knew a Catholic girl that married an old Protestant three times her own age. I entreated her not to do so; but it was useless. And when the disillusionment came she used to write to me piteous letters, telling me that her husband had in reality no religion at all. He was a convinced infidel, and scouted even the idea of the soul's immortality.

"After two years of married life the old man died. He was about sixty years old; but very hale and hearty till the end.

"Well, when he took to his bed, the wife sent for me, and I had half a dozen interviews with him; but it was useless. He told me plainly that he wanted to believe—in fact he said that the thought of annihilation was intolerable to him. If he had had a child he would not have hated death so much; if his flesh and blood in any manner survived him, he could have fancied that he had a sort of vicarious life left; but as it was there was no kith or kin of his alive; and he could not bear that."

Father Macclesfield sniffed cynically, and folded his hands.

"I may say that his death-bed was extremely unpleasant. He was a coarse old fellow, with plenty of strength in him; and he used to make remarks about the churchyard— and—and in fact the worms, that used to send his poor child of a wife half fainting out of the room. He had lived an immoral life too, I gathered.

"Just at the last it was—well—disgusting. He had no consideration. (God knows why she married him!) The agony was a very long one; he caught at the curtains round the bed; calling out; and all his words were about death, and the dark. It seemed to me that he caught hold of the curtains as if to hold himself into this world. And at the very end he raised himself clean up in bed, and stared horribly out of the window that was open just opposite.

"I must tell you that straight away beneath the window lay a long walk, between sheets of dead leaves with laurels on either side, and the branches meeting overhead, so that it was very dark there even in summer; and at the end of the walk away from the house was the churchyard gate."

Father Macclesfield paused and blew his nose. Then he went on still without looking at us.

"Well, the old man died; and he was carried along this laurel path, and buried.

"His wife was in such a state that I simply dared not go away. She was frightened to death; and, indeed, the whole affair of her husband's dying was horrible. But she would not leave the house. She had a fancy that it would be cruel to him. She used to go down twice a day to pray at the grave; but she never went along the laurel walk. She would go round by the garden and in at a lower gate, and come back the same way, or by the upper garden.

"This went on for three or four days. The man had died on a Saturday, and was buried on Monday; it was in July; and he had died about eight o'clock.

"I made up my mind to go on the Saturday after the funeral. My curate had managed along very well for a few days; but I did not like to leave him for a second Sunday.

"Then on the Friday at lunch—her sister had come down, by the way, and was still in the house—on the Friday the widow said something about never daring to sleep in the room where the old man had died. I told her it was nonsense, and so on; but you must remember she was in a dreadful state of nerves, and she persisted. So I said I would sleep in the room myself. I had no patience with such ideas then.

"Of course she said all sorts of things, but I had my way; and my things were moved in on Friday evening.

"I went to my new room about a quarter before eight to put on my cassock for dinner. The room was very much as it had been—rather dark because of the trees at the end of the walk outside. There was the four-poster there with the damask curtains; the table and chairs, the cupboard where his clothes were kept, and so on.

"When I had put my cassock on, I went to the window to look out. To right and left were the gardens, with the sunlight just off them, but still very bright and gay, with the geraniums, and exactly opposite was the laurel walk, like a long green shady tunnel, dividing the upper and lower lawns.

"I could see straight down it to the churchyard gate, which was about a hundred yards away, I suppose. There were limes overhead, and laurels, as I said, on each side.

"Well—I saw someone coming up the walk; but it seemed to me at first that he was drunk. He staggered several times as I watched; I suppose he would be fifty yards away—and once I saw him catch hold of one of the trees and cling against it as if he were afraid of falling. Then he left it, and came on again slowly, going from side to side, with his hands out. He seemed desperately keen to get to the house.

"I could see his dress; and it astonished me that a man dressed so should be drunk; for he was quite plainly a gentleman. He wore a white top hat, and a grey cut-away coat, and grey trousers, and I could make out his white spats.

"Then it struck me he might be ill; and I looked harder than ever, wondering whether I ought to go down.

"When he was about twenty yards away he lifted his face; and, it struck me as very odd, but it seemed to me he was extraordinarily like the old man we had buried on Monday; but it was darkish where he was, and the next moment he dropped his face, threw up his hands and fell flat on his back.

"Well, of course I was startled at that, and I leaned out of the window and called out something. He was moving his hands I could see, as if he were in convulsions; and I could hear the dry leaves rustling.

"Well, then I turned and ran out and downstairs."

Father Macclesfield stopped a moment.

"Gentlemen," he said abruptly, "when I got there, there was not a sign of the old man. I could see that the leaves had been disturbed, but that was all."

There was an odd silence in the room as he paused; but before any of us had time to speak he went on.

"Of course I did not say a word of what I had seen. We dined as usual; I smoked for an hour or so by myself after prayers; and then I went up to bed. I cannot say I was perfectly comfortable, for I was not; but neither was I frightened.

"When I got to my room I lit all my candles, and then went to a big cupboard I had noticed, and pulled out some of the drawers. In the bottom of the third drawer I found a grey cutaway coat and grey trousers; I found several pairs of white spats in the top drawer; and a white hat on the shelf above. That is the first incident."

"Did you sleep there, Father?" said a voice softly.

"I did," said the priest; "there was no reason why I should not. I did not fall asleep for two or three hours; but I was not disturbed in any way; and came to breakfast as usual.

"Well, I thought about it all a bit; and finally I sent a wire to my curate telling him I was detained. I did not like to leave the house just then."

Father Macclesfield settled himself again in his chair and went on, in the same dry uninterested voice.

"On Sunday we drove over to the Catholic Church, six miles off, and I said Mass. Nothing more happened till the Monday evening.

"That evening I went to the window again about a quarter before eight, as I had done both on the Saturday and Sunday. Everything was perfectly quiet, till I heard the churchyard gate unlatch; and I saw a man come through.

"But I saw almost at once that it was not the same man I had seen before; it looked to me like a keeper, for he had a gun across his arm; then I saw him hold the gate open an instant, and a dog came through and began to trot up the path towards the house with his master following.

"When the dog was about fifty yards away he stopped dead, and pointed.

"I saw the keeper throw his gun forward and come up softly; and as he came the dog began to slink backwards. I watched very closely, clean forgetting why I was there; and the next instant something—it was too shadowy under the trees to see exactly what it was—but something about the size of a hare burst out of the laurels and made straight up the path, dodging from side to side, but coming like the wind.

"The beast could not have been more than twenty yards from me, when the keeper fired, and the creature went over and over in the dry leaves, and lay struggling and screaming.

It was horrible! But what astonished me was that the dog did not come up. I heard the keeper snap out something, and then I saw the dog making off down the avenue in the direction of the churchyard as hard as he could go.

"The keeper was running now towards me; but the screaming of the hare, or of whatever it was, had stopped; and I was astonished to see the man come right up to where the beast was struggling and kicking, and then stop as if he was puzzled.

"I leaned out of the window and called to him.

"'Right in front of you, man,' I said. 'For God's sake kill the brute.'

"He looked up at me, and then down again.

"'Where is it, sir,' he said. 'I can't see it anywhere.'

"And there lay the beast clear before him all the while, not a yard away, still kicking.

"Well, I went out of the room and downstairs and out to the avenue.

"The man was standing there still, looking terribly puzzled, but the hare was gone. There was not a sign of it. Only the leaves were disturbed, and the wet earth showed beneath.

"The keeper said that it had been a great hare; he could have sworn to it; and that he had orders to kill all hares and rabbits in the garden enclosure. Then he looked rather odd.

"'Did you see it plainly, sir?' he asked.

"I told him, not very plainly, but I thought it a hare too.

"'Yes, sir,' he said, 'it was a hare, sure enough; but, do you know, sir, I thought it to be a kind of silver grey with white feet. I never saw one like that before!'

"The odd thing was that not a dog would come near, his own dog was gone; but I fetched the yard dog—a retriever, out of his kennel in the kitchen yard, and if ever I saw a frightened dog it was this one. When we dragged him up at last, all whining and pulling back, he began to snap at us so fiercely that we let go, and he went back like the wind to his kennel. It was the same with the terrier.

"Well, the bell had gone, and I had to go in and explain why I was late; but I didn't say anything about the colour of the hare. That was the second incident."

Father Macclesfield stopped again, smiling reminiscently to himself. I was very much impressed by his quiet air and composure. I think it helped his story a good deal.

Again, before we had time to comment or question he went on.

"The third incident was so slight that I should not have mentioned it, or thought anything of it, if it had not been for the others; but it seemed to me there was a kind of diminishing gradation of energy, which explained. Well, now you shall hear.

"On the other nights of that week I was at my window again; but nothing happened till the Friday. I had arranged to go for certain next day; the widow was much better and more reasonable, and even talked of going abroad herself in the following week.

"On that Friday evening I dressed a little earlier, and went down to the avenue this time, instead of staying at my window, at about twenty minutes to eight.

"It was rather a heavy depressing evening, without a breath of wind, and darker than it had been for some days.

"I walked slowly down the avenue to the gate and back again; and, I suppose it was fancy, but I felt more uncomfortable than I had felt at all up to then. I was rather relieved to see the widow come out of the house and stand looking down the avenue. I came out myself then and went towards her. She started rather when she saw me and then smiled.

"'I thought it was someone else,' she said. 'Father, I have made up my mind to go. I shall go to town tomorrow, and start on Monday. My sister will come with me.'

"I congratulated her; and then we turned and began to walk back to the lime avenue. She stopped at the entrance, and seemed unwilling to come any further.

"'Come down to the end,' I said, 'and back again. There will be time before dinner.'

"She said nothing; but came with me; and we went straight down to the gate and then turned to come back.

"I don't think either of us spoke a word; I was very uncomfortable indeed by now; and yet I had to go on.

"We were halfway back I suppose when I heard a sound like a gate rattling; and I whisked round in an instant, expecting to see someone at the gate. But there was no one.

"Then there came a rustling overhead in the leaves; it had been dead still before. Then I don't know why, but I took my friend suddenly by the arm and drew her to one side out of the path, so that we stood on the right hand, not a foot from the laurels.

"She said nothing, and I said nothing; but I think we were both looking this way and that, as if we expected to see something.

"The breeze died, and then sprang up again; but it was

only a breath. I could hear the living leaves rustling over-head, and the dead leaves underfoot; and it was blowing gently from the churchyard.

"Then I saw a thing that one often sees; but I could not take my eyes off it, nor could she. It was a little column of leaves, twisting and turning and dropping and picking up again in the wind, coming slowly up the path. It was a capricious sort of draught, for the little scurry of leaves went this way and that, to and fro across the path. It came up to us, and I could feel the breeze on my hands and face. One leaf struck me softly on the cheek, and I can only say that I shuddered as if it had been a toad. Then it passed on.

"You understand, gentlemen, it was pretty dark; but it seemed to me that the breeze died and the column of leaves—it was no more than a little twist of them—sank down at the end of the avenue.

"We stood there perfectly still for a moment or two; and when I turned, she was staring straight at me, but nei-ther of us said one word.

"We did not go up the avenue to the house. We pushed our way through the laurels, and came back by the upper garden.

"Nothing else happened; and the next morning we all went off by the eleven o'clock train.

"That is all, gentlemen."

XII

Father Stein's Tale

OLD Father Stein was a figure that greatly fascinated me during my first weeks in Rome, after I had got over the slight impatience that his personality roused in me. He was slow of speech and thought and movement, and had that distressing grip of the obvious that is characteristic of the German mind. I soon rejoiced to look at his heavy face, generally unshaven, his deep twinkling eyes, and the ponderous body that had such an air of eternal immovability, and to watch his mind, as through a glass case, labouring like an engine over a fact that he had begun to assimilate. He took a kind of paternal interest in me too, and would thrust his thick hand under my arm as he stood by me, or clap me heavily on the shoulder as we met. But he was excellently educated, had seen much of the world, although always through a haze of the Fatherland that accompanied him everywhere, and had acquired an exceptional knowledge of English during his labours in a London mission. He used his large vocabulary with a good deal of skill.

I was pleased then when Monsignor announced on the following evening that Father Stein was prepared to contribute a story. But the German, knowing that he was master of the situation, would utter nothing at first but hoarse ejaculations at the thought of his reminiscences, and it was not until we had been seated for nearly half an hour before the fire that he consented to begin.

"It is of a dream," he said, "no more than that; and yet dreams too are under the hand of the good God—so I hold. Some, I know, are just folly, and tell us of nothing but the confusion of our own nature when the controlling will is withdrawn; but some, I hold, are the whispers of God and tell us of what we are too dull to hear in our waking life. You do not believe me? Very well, then. Listen.

"I knew a man in Germany, thirty years ago, who had lived many years away from God. He had been a Catholic, and was well-educated in religion till he grew to be a lad. Then he fell into sin, and dared not confess it; and he lied, and made bad confessions and approached the altar so. He once went to a strange priest to tell his sin, and dared not when the time came; and so added sin to sin, and lost his faith. It is ever so. We know it well. The soul dare not go on in that state, believing in God; and so by an inner act of the will renounces Him. It is not true, it is not true, she cries; and at last the voice of faith is silent, and her eyes blind."

The priest stopped and looked round him, and the old Rector nodded once or twice and murmured assent.

"For twenty years he had lived so; without God, and he was not unhappy; for the powers of his soul died one by one and he could no longer feel. Once or twice they struggled, in their death agony, and he stamped on them again. Once when his mother died, he nearly lived again; and his soul cried once more within him, and stirred herself; but he would not hear her; it is useless, he said to her, there is no hope for you; lie still, there is nothing for you; you are dreaming; there is no life such as you think; and he trampled her again, and she lay still."

We were all very quiet now; I certainly had not suspected such passion in this old priest; he had seemed to me slow and dull and not capable of any sort of delicate thought or phrase, far less of tragedy; but somehow now his great face was lighted up, his eyebrows twitched as he talked; and it seemed as if we were hearing of a murder that this man had seen for himself. Monsignor sat perfectly motionless staring intently into the fire; Father Brent was watching the German sideways; Father Stein took a deliberate pinch of snuff, snapped his box, and put it away, and went on.

"This man had lived on the sea-coast as a child, but was now in business in a town on the Rhine; and had never visited his old home since he left it with his mother on his father's death. He was now about thirty-five years of age, when God was gracious to him. He was living in a cousin's house, with whom he was partner.

"One night he dreamed he was a child, and walking with one whom he knew was his sister who had died before he was born; but he could not see her face. They were on a white dusty road, and it was the noon of a hot summer day. There was nothing to be seen round him, but great slopes of a dusty country with dry grass; and the burning sky overhead, and the sun. He was tired, and his feet ached, and he was crying as he walked, but he dared not cry loud for fear that his sister would turn and look at him, and he knew she was a——a *revenant* and did not wish to see her eyes. There was no wind, and no birds, and no clouds; only the grasshoppers sawed in the dry grass, and the blood drummed in his ears until he thought he would go mad with the noise. And so they walked, the boy behind his sister, up a long hill. It seemed to him that they had been walking so for hours, for a lifetime; and that there would be no end to it. His feet sank to the ankles in dust, the sun beat on to his brain from above, the white road glared from below; and the tears ran down his cheeks.

"Then there was a breath of salt wind in his face, and his sister began to go faster, noiselessly; and he tried too to go faster, but could not; his heart beat like a hammer in his throat, and his feet lagged more and more; and little by little his sister was far in front; and he dared not cry out to her not to leave him, for fear she should turn and look at him; and at last he was walking alone; and he dared not lie down or rest.

"The road passed up a slope, and when he reached the top of it at last, he saw her again, far away, a little figure that turned to him and waved its hand; and behind her was the blue sea, very faint and in a mist of heat; and then he knew that the end of the bitter journey was very near.

"As he passed up the last slope the sea-line rose higher against the sky, but the line was only as the fine mark of a pencil where sea and sky met, and a dazzling white bird or two passed across it, and then dropped below the cliff. By the time he came near his sister the dusty road had died away into the grass, and he was walking over the fresh turf that felt cool to his hot feet. He threw himself down on the edge of it, by his sister, where she was lying with her head on her hands looking out at the sea where it spread itself out, a thousand feet below; and still he had not seen her face.

"At the foot of the cliff was a little white beach, and the rocks ran down into deep water on every side of it, and threw a purple shadow across the sand; and there were birds here too, floating out from the cliff and turning and returning; and the sea beneath them was a clear blue, like a Cardinal's ring that I saw once; and the breeze blew up from the water and made him happy again."

Father Stein stopped again, with something of a sob in his old heavy voice; and then he turned to us.

"You know such dreams," he said, "I cannot tell it as—as he told me; but he said it was like the bliss of the redeemed to look down on the sea and feel the breeze in his hair, and taste its saltness.

"He did not wish his sister to speak, though he was afraid of her no more; and yet he knew that there was some secret to be told that would explain all—why they were here, and why she had come back to him, and why the sea was here, and the little beach below them, and the wind and the birds. But he was content to wait until it was time for her to tell him, as he knew she would. It was enough to be here, after the dusty journey, beside her, and to wait for the word that should be spoken.

"Now at first he was so out of breath, and his heart beat so in his ears, that he could hear nothing but that and his own panting; but it grew quieter soon, and he began to hear something else—the noises of the sea beneath him. It was a still day, but there was movement down below; and the surge heaved itself softly against the cliff, and murmured in deep caves below, like the pedal note of the Frankfort organ, solemn and splendid; and the waves leaned over and crashed gently on the sand. It was all so far beneath that he saw the breaking wave before the sound came up to him; and he lay there and watched and listened; and that great sound made him happier even than the light on the water, and the coolness and rest; for it was the sea itself that was speaking now.

"Then he saw suddenly that his sister had turned on her elbow and was looking at him; and he looked into her eyes, and knew her, though she had died before he was born. And she too was listening with her lips parted to the sound of the surge. And now he knew that the secret was to be told; and he watched her eyes, smiling. And she lifted her hand, as if to hold him silent, and waited; and again the sweet murmur and crash rose up from the sea; and she spoke, softly.

"'It is the Precious Blood,' she said."

Father Stein was silent; and we all were silent for a while. As far as I was concerned at least the story had somehow held me with an extraordinary fascination, I scarcely knew why.

There was a movement among the others, and present-ly the Frenchman spoke.

"*Et puis?*" he said.

"The man awoke," said Father Stein, "and found tears on his face."

It was such a short story that there were still a few minutes before the time for night prayers, and we sat there without speaking again until the clock sounded in the campanile overhead, and the Rector rose and led the way into the West gallery of the church. I saw Father Stein waiting at the door for me to come up, and I knew why he was waiting.

He took my arm in his thick hand and held it a moment as the others passed down the two steps. Then he pressed it, and I understood what he meant.

XIII

Mr. Percival's Tale

WHEN I came in from Mass into the refectory on the morning following Father Stein's story, I found a layman breakfasting there with the Father Rector. We were introduced to one another; and I learned that Mr. Percival was a barrister who had arrived from England that morning on a holiday and was to stay at S. Filippo for a fortnight.

I yield to none in my respect for the clergy. At the same time a layman feels occasionally something of a pariah among them. I suppose this is bound to be so, so I was pleased then to find another dog of my breed with whom I might consort, and even howl, if I so desired. I was pleased, too, with his appearance. He had that trim academic air that is characteristic of the Bar, in spite of his twenty-two hours' journey, and was dressed in an excellently made grey suit. He was very slightly bald on his forehead, and had those sharp-cut mask-like features that mark a man as either lawyer, priest, or actor; he had besides delightful manners and even, white teeth. I do not think I could have suggested any improvements in person, behaviour, or costume.

By the time that my coffee had arrived, the Father Rector had run dry of conversation and I could see that he was relieved when I joined in.

In a few minutes I was telling Mr. Percival about the symposium we had formed for the relating of preternatural adventures; and I presently asked him whether he had ever had any experience of the kind.

He shook his head.

"I have not," he said in his virile voice; "my business takes my time."

"I wish you had been with us earlier," put in the Rector. "I think you would have been interested."

"I am sure of it," he said. "I remember once—but you know, Father, frankly I am something of a sceptic."

"You remember—?" I suggested.

He smiled very pleasantly with eyes and mouth.

"Yes, Mr. Benson. I was once next door to such a story. A friend of mine saw something; but I was not with him at the moment."

"Well, we thought we had finished last night," I said, "but do you think you would be too tired to entertain us this evening?"

"I shall be delighted to tell the story," he said easily. "But indeed I am a sceptic in this matter; I cannot dress it up."

"We want the naked fact," I said.

I went sight-seeing with him that day, and found him extremely intelligent and at the same time accurate. The two virtues do not run often together; and I felt confident that whatever he chose to tell us would be salient and true. I felt, too, that he would need few questions to draw him out; he would say what there was to be said unaided.

When we had taken our places that night, he began by again apologizing for his attitude of mind.

"I do not know, Reverend Fathers," he said, "what are

your own theories in this matter; but it appears to me that if what seems to be preternatural can possibly be brought within the range of the natural, one is bound scientifically to treat it in that way. Now in this story of mine—for I will give you a few words of explanation first in order to prejudice your minds as much as possible; in this story the whole matter might be accounted for by the imagination. My friend who saw what he saw was under rather theatrical circumstances, and he is an Irishman. Besides that, he knew the history of the place in which he was; and he was quite alone. On the other hand, he has never had an experience of the kind before or since; he is perfectly truthful, and he saw what he saw in moderate daylight. I give you these facts first, and I think you would be perfectly justified in thinking they account for everything. As for my own theory, which is not quite that, I have no idea whether you will agree or disagree with it. I do not say that my judgment is the only sensible one, or anything offensive like that. I merely state what I feel I am bound to accept for the present."

There was a murmur of assent. Then he crossed his legs, leaned back and began:

"In my first summer after I was called to the Bar I went down South Wales for a holiday with another man who had been with me at Oxford. His name was Murphy: he is a J.P. now, in Ireland, I think. I cannot think why we went to South Wales—but there it is: we did.

"We took the train to Cardiff, sent on our luggage up the Taff Valley to an inn of which I cannot remember the name—but it was close to where Lord Bute has a vineyard. Then we walked up to Llandaff, saw St. Tylo's tomb, and went on again to this village.

"Next morning we thought we would look about us before going on, and we went out for a stroll. It was one of the most glorious mornings I ever remember, quite cloudless and very hot; and we went up through woods to get a breeze at the top of the hill.

"We found that the whole place was full of iron mines, disused now, as the iron is richer further up the country; but I can tell you that they enormously improved the interest of the place. We found shaft after shaft, some protected and some not, but mostly overgrown with bushes, so we had to walk carefully. We had passed half a dozen, I should think, before the thought of going down one of them occurred to Murphy.

"Well, we got down one at last—though I rather wished for a rope once or twice—and I think it was one of the most extraordinary sights I have ever seen. You know perhaps what the cave of a demon-king is like, in the first act of a pantomime. Well, it was like that. There was a kind of blue light that poured down the shafts, refracted from surface to surface, so that the sky was invisible. On all sides passages ran into total darkness; huge reddish rocks stood out fantastically everywhere in the pale light; there was a sound of water falling into a pool from a great height and presently, striking matches as we went, we came upon a couple of lakes of marvellously clear blue water through which we could see the heads of ladders emerging from other black holes of unknown depth below.

"We found our way out after a while into what appeared to be the central hall of the mine. Here we saw plain daylight again, for there was an immense round opening at the top, from the edges of which curved away the sides of the shaft, forming a huge circular chamber.

"Imagine the Albert Hall roofless; or better still, imagine Saint Peter's with the top half of the dome removed. Of course it was far smaller, but it gave an impression of great size, and it could not have been less than two hundred feet from the edge, over which we saw the trees against the sky, to the tumbled dusty rocky floor where we stood.

"I can only describe it as being like a great, burnt-out hell in the *Inferno*. Red dust lay everywhere, escape seemed impossible; and vast crags and galleries, with the mouths of passages showing high up, marked by iron bars and chains, jutted out here and there.

"We amused ourselves here for some time, by climbing up the sides, calling to one another, for the whole place was full of echoes, rolling down stones from some of the upper ledges: but I nearly ended my days there.

"I was standing on a path, about seventy feet up, leaning against the wall. It was a path along which feet must have gone a thousand times when the mine was in working order; and I was watching Murphy who was just emerging on to a platform opposite me, on the other side of the gulf.

"I put my hand behind me to steady myself, and the next instant very nearly fell forward over the edge at the violent shock to my nerves given by a wood-pigeon who burst out of a hole, brushing my hand as he passed. I gripped on, however, and watched the bird soar out across space, and then up and out at the opening; and then I became aware that my knees were beginning to shake. So I stumbled along, and threw myself down on the little platform on to which the passage led.

"I suppose I had been more startled than I knew; for I tripped as I went forward; and knocked my knee rather sharply on a stone. I felt for an instant quite sick with the pain on the top of jangling nerves; and lay there saying what I am afraid I ought not to have said.

"Then Murphy came up when I called, and we made our way together through one of the sloping shafts, and came out on to the hillside among the trees."

Mr. Percival paused; his lips twitched a moment with amusement.

"I am afraid I must recall my promise," he said. "I told you all this because I was anxious to give a reason for the feeling I had about the mine, and which I am bound to mention. I felt I never wanted to see the place again—yet in spite of what followed I do not necessarily attribute my feelings to anything but the shock and the pain that I had had. You understand that?"

His bright eyes ran round our faces.

"Yes, yes," said Monsignor sharply, "go on, please, Mr. Percival."

"Well, then!"

The lawyer uncrossed his legs and replaced them the other way.

"During lunch we told the landlady where we had been, and she begged us not to go there again. I told her that she might rest easy: my knee was beginning to swell. It was a wretched beginning to a walking tour.

"It was not that, she said, but there had been a bad accident there. Four men had been killed there twenty years before by a fall of rock. That had been the last straw on the top of ill-success, and the mine had been abandoned.

"We inquired as to details, and it seemed that the accident had taken place in the central chamber, locally called 'The Cathedral'; and after a few more questions I understood.

"'That was where you were, my friend,' I said to Murphy, 'it was where you were when the bird flew out.'

"He agreed with me, and presently when the woman was gone announced that he was going to the mine again to see the place. Well, I had no business to keep him dangling about. I couldn't walk anywhere myself, so I advised him not to go on to that platform again; and presently he took a couple of candles from the sticks and went off. He promised to be back by four o'clock, and I settled down rather drearily to a pipe and some old magazines.

"Naturally I fell sound asleep. It was a hot, drowsy afternoon and the magazines were dull. I awoke once or twice, and then slept again deeply.

"I was awakened by the woman coming in to ask whether I would have tea—it was already five o'clock. I told her Yes. I was not in the least anxious about Murphy; he was a good climber, and therefore neither a coward nor a fool.

"As tea came in I looked out of the window again, and saw him walking up to the path, covered with iron-dust, and a moment later I heard his step in the passage; and he came in.

"Mrs. What's-her-name had gone out.

"'Have you had a good time?' I asked.

"He looked at me very oddly, and paused before he answered.

"'Oh, yes,' he said; and put his cap and stick in a corner.

"I knew Murphy.

"'Well, why not?' I asked him, beginning to pour out tea.

"He looked round at the door, then he sat down without noticing the cup I pushed across to him.

"'My dear fellow,' he said. 'I think I am going mad.'

"Well, I forget what I said, but I understood that he was very much upset about something, and I suppose I said the proper kind of thing about his not being a qualified fool.

"Then he told me his story."

Mr. Percival looked round at us again, still with that slight twitching of the lips that seemed to signify amusement.

"Please remember—" he began, and then broke off. "No—I won't—"

"Well. He had gone down the same shaft that we went down in the morning; and had spent a couple of hours exploring the passages. He had found an engine room with tanks and rotten beams in it, and rusty chains. He had found some more lakes too, full of that extraordinary electric-blue water; he had disturbed a quantity of bats somewhere else. Then he had come out again into the central hall, and on looking at his watch had found it after four o'clock, so he thought he would climb up by the way we had come in the morning and go straight home.

"It was as he climbed that his odd sensations began. As he went up, clinging with his hands, he became perfectly certain that he was being watched. He couldn't turn round very well; but he looked up as he went to the opening overhead, but there was nothing there but the dead blue sky, and the trees very green against it, and the red rocks curving away on every side. It was extraordinarily quiet, he said, the pigeons had not come home from feeding, and he was out of hearing of the dripping water that I told you of.

"Then he reached the platform and the opening of the path where I had had my fright in the morning, and turned round to look.

"At first he saw nothing peculiar. The rocks up which he had come fell away at his feet down to the floor of the 'Cathedral' and to the nettles with which he had stung his hands a minute or two before. He looked around at the galleries overhead and opposite; but there was nothing there.

"Then he looked across at the platform where he had been in the morning and where the accident had taken place.

"Let me tell you what this was like. It was about twenty yards in breadth, and ten deep; but lay irregular, and filled with tumbled rocks. It was a little below the level of his eyes, right across the gulf; and, in a straight line, would be about fifty or sixty yards away. It lay under the roof, rather retired, so that no light from the sky fell directly on to it; it would have been in complete twilight if it hadn't been for a shaft smaller above it, which shot down a funnel of bluish light, exactly like a stage-effect. You see, Reverend Fathers, it was very theatrical altogether. That might account no doubt—"

Mr. Percival broke off again, smiling.

"I am always forgetting," he said. "Well, we must go back to Murphy. At first he saw nothing but the rocks, and the thick red dust, and the broken wall behind it. He was very honest, and told me that as he looked at it, he remembered distinctly what the landlady had told us at lunch. It was on that little stage that the tragedy had happened.

"Then he became aware that something was moving among the rocks, and he became perfectly certain that people were looking at him; but it was too dusky to see very clearly at first. Whatever it was, was in the shadows at the back. He fixed his eyes on what was moving. Then this happened."

The lawyer stopped again.

"I will tell you the rest," he said, "in his own words, so far as I remember them.

"'I was looking at this moving thing,' he said, 'which seemed exactly of the red colour of the rocks, when it suddenly came out under the funnel of light; and I saw it was a man. He was in a rough suit, all iron-stained; with a rusty cap; and he had some kind of a pick in his hand. He stopped first in the centre of the light, with his back turned to me, and stood there, looking. I cannot say that I was consciously frightened; I honestly do not know what I thought he was. I think that my whole mind was taken up in watching him.

" 'Then he turned round slowly, and I saw his face. Then I became aware that if he looked at me I should go into hysterics or something of the sort; and I crouched down as low as I could. But he didn't look at me; he was attending to something else; and I could see his face quite clearly. He had a beard and moustache, rather ragged and rusty; he was rather pale, but not particularly; I judged him to be about thirty-five.' Of course," went on the lawyer, "Murphy didn't tell it me quite as I am telling it to you. He stopped a good deal, he drank a sip of tea once or twice, and changed his feet about.

"Well, he had seen this man's face very clearly, and described it very clearly.

"It was the expression that struck him most.

" 'It was a rather amused expression,' he said, 'rather pathetic and rather tender; and he was looking interestedly about at everything—at the rocks above and beneath: he carried his pick easily in the crook of his arm. He looked exactly like a man whom I once saw visiting his home where he had lived as a child.' (Murphy was very particular about that, though I don't believe he was right.) 'He was smiling a little in his beard, and his eyes were half-shut. It was so pathetic that I nearly went into hysterics then and there,' said Murphy. 'I wanted to stand up and explain that it was all right, but I knew he knew more than I did. I watched him, I should think for nearly five minutes, he went to and fro softly in the thick dust, looking here and there, sometimes in the shadow and sometimes out of it. I could not have moved for ten thousand pounds, and I could not take my eyes off him.

"'Then just before the end, I did look away from him. I wanted to know if it was all real, and I looked at the rocks behind and the openings. Then I saw that there were other people there, at least there were things moving, of the colour of the rocks.

"'I suppose I made some sound then; I was horribly frightened. At any rate, the man in the middle turned right round and faced me, and at that I sank down, with the sweat dripping from me, flat on my face, with my hands over my eyes.

"'I thought of a hundred thousand things: of the inn, and you; and the walk we had had—and I prayed—well, I suppose I prayed. I wanted God to take me right out of this place. I wanted the rocks to open and let me through.'"

Mr. Percival stopped. His voice shook with a tiny tremor. He cleared his throat.

"Well, Reverend Fathers, Murphy got up at last, and looked about him, and of course there was nothing there, but just the rocks and the dust, and the sky overhead. Then he came away home, the shortest way."

It was a very abrupt ending; and a little sigh ran round the circle. Monsignor struck a match noisily, and kindled his pipe again.

"Thank you very much, sir," he said briskly.

Mr. Percival cleared his throat again, but before he could speak Father Brent broke in.

"Now that is just an instance of what I was saying, Monsignor, the night we began. May I ask if you really believe that those were the souls of the miners? Where's the justice of it? What's the point?"

Monsignor glanced at the lawyer.

"Have you any theory, sir? "he asked.

Mr. Percival answered without lifting his eyes.

"I think so," he said shortly, "but I don't feel in the least dogmatic."

Father Brent looked at him almost indignantly. "I should like to hear it," he said, "if you can square that—"

"I do not square it," said the lawyer. "Personally I do not believe they were spirits at all."

"Oh?"

"No, I do not—though I do not wish to be dogmatic. To my mind it seems far more likely that this is an instance of Mr. Hudson's theory—the American, you know. His idea is that all apparitions are no more than the result of violent emotions experienced during life. That about the pathetic expression is all nonsense, I believe."

"I don't understand," said Father Brent.

"Well, these men, killed by the fall of the roof, probably went through a violent emotion. This would be heightened in some degree by their loneliness and isolation from the world. This kind of emotion, Mr. Hudson suggests, has a power of saturating material surroundings and which, under certain circumstances would once more, like a phonograph, give off an image of the agent. In this instance, too, the absence of other human visitors would give this materialized emotion a chance, so to speak, of surviving: there would be very few cross-currents to confuse it. And finally, Murphy was alone; his receptive faculties would be stimulated by that fact, and all that he saw, in my belief, was the psychical wave left by these men in dying."

"Oh! Did you tell him so?"

"I did not. Murphy is a violent man."

I looked up at Monsignor, and saw him nodding emphatically to himself.

XIV

My Own Tale

I must confess that I was a little taken aback, on my last evening before leaving for England, when Monsignor Maxwell turned on me suddenly at supper, and exclaimed aloud that I had not yet contributed a story.

I protested that I had none; that I was a prosaic person; that there was some packing to be done; that my business was to write down the stories of other people; that I had my living to make and could not be liberal with my slender store; that it was a layman's function to sit at holy and learned priests' feet, not to presume to inform them on any subject under the sun.

But it was impossible to resist; it was pointed out to me that I had listened on false pretences if I had not intended to do my share, that telling a story did not hinder my printing it. And as a final argument it was declared that unless I occupied the chair that night, all present withdrew the leave that had already been given to me to print their stories on my return to England.

There was nothing therefore to be done; and as I had already considered the possibility of the request, I did not occupy an unduly long time in pretending to remember what I had to say.

When I was seated upstairs, and the fire had been poked according to the ritual, and the matches had gone round, and buckled shoes protruded side by side with elastic-ankled boots, I began.

"This is a very unsatisfactory story," I said, "because it has no explanation of any kind. It is quite unlike Mr. Percival's. You will see that even theorizing is useless, when I have come to the end. It is simply a series of facts that I have to relate, facts that have no significance except one that is supernatural; but it is utterly out of the question even to guess at that significance.

"It is unsatisfactory, too, for a second reason; and that is, that it is on such very hackneyed lines. It is simply one more instance of that very dreary class of phenomena, named haunted houses; except that there is no ghost in it. Its only claim to interest is, as I have said, the complete futility of any attempt to explain it."

This was rather a pompous exordium, I felt; but I thought it best not to raise expectations too high, and I was therefore deliberately dull.

"Sixteen years ago from last summer, I was in Brittany. I had left school where I had laboured two hours a week at French for four years; and gone away in order to learn it in six weeks. This I accomplished very tolerably, in company with five other boys and an English tutor. Our general adventures are not relevant; but toward the end of our stay we went over one Sunday from Portrieux in order to see a French château about three miles away.

"It was a really glorious June day, hot and fresh and exhilarating; and we lunched delightfully in the woods with a funny fat little French Count and his wife who came with us from the hotel. It is impossible to imagine less uncanny circumstances or companions.

"After lunch we all went cheerfully to the house, whose chimneys we had seen among the trees.

"I know nothing about the dates of houses; but the sort of impression I got of this house was that it was about three hundred years old; yet it may equally have been four, or two. I did not know then, and do not know now, anything about it except its name, which I will not tell you; and its owner's name which I will not tell you either—and—and something else that I will tell you. We will call the owner, if you please, Comte Jean Marie the First. The house is built in two courts. The right-hand court through which we entered was then used as a farmyard; and I should think it probable that it is still so used. This court was exceedingly untidy. There was a large manure heap in the centre; and the servants' quarters to our right looked miserably cared for. There was a cart or two with shafts turned up, near the sheds that were built against the wall opposite the gate; and there was a sleepy old dog with bleared eyes that looked at us crossly from his kennel door.

"Our French friend went across to the servants' cottages with his moustache sticking out on either side of his face, and presently came back with two girls and the keys. There was no objection, he exclaimed dramatically, to our seeing the house!

"The girls went before us, and unlocked the iron gate that led to the second court; and we went through after them.

"Now, we had heard at the hotel that the family lived

in Paris; but we were not prepared for the dreadful desolation of that inner court. The living part of the house was on our left; and what had once been a lawn to our right; but the house was discoloured and weather-stained; the green paint of the closed shutters and door was cracked and blistered; and the lawn resembled a wilderness; the grass was long and rank; there were rose trees trailing along the edge and across the path; and a sun dial on the lawn reminded me strangely of a drunken man petrified in the middle of a stagger. All this of course was what was to be expected in an adventure of this kind. It would do for a Christmas number.

"But it was not our business to criticize; and after a moment or two, we followed the girls who had unlocked the front door and were waiting for us to enter.

"One of them had gone before to open the shutters.

"It was not a large house, in spite of its name; and we had soon looked through the lower rooms of it. They, too, were what you would expect: the floors were beeswaxed; there were tables and chairs of a tolerable antiquity; a little damask on the walls, and so on. But what astonished us was the fact that none of the furniture was covered up, or even moved aside; and the dust lay, I should say, half-an-inch thick on every horizontal surface. I heard the Frenchman crying on his God in an undertone—as is the custom of Gauls"—I bowed a little to Father Meuron—"and finally he burst out with a question as to why the rooms were in this state.

"The girl looked at him stolidly. She was a stout, red-faced girl.

"'It is by the Count's orders,' she said.

"'And does the Count not come here?' he asked.

"'No, sir.'

"'Then we all went upstairs. One of the girls had preceded us again and was waiting with her hand on the door to usher us in.

"'See here the room, the most splendid,' she said, and threw the door open.

"It was certainly the room most splendid. It was a great bed-chamber, hung with tapestry; there were some excellent chairs with carved legs; a fine gold framed mirror tilted forward over the carved mantel-piece; and, above all, and standing out from the wall opposite the window was a great four-posted bed, with an elaborately carved head to it, and heavy curtains hanging from the canopy.

"But what surprised us more than anything that we had yet seen, was the sight of the bed. Except for the dust that lay on it, it might have been slept in the night before. There were actually damask sheets upon it, thrown back, and two pillows—all grey with dust. These were not arranged but tumbled about, as a bed is in the morning before it is made.

"As I was looking at this, I heard a boy cry out from the washing-stand:

"'Why it has had water in it,' he said.

"This did not sound exceptional for a basin, but we all crowded round to look; and it was perfectly true; there was a grey film around the interior of it; and when he had disturbed it (as a boy would) with his finger, we could see the flowered china beneath. The line came two-thirds of the way up the sides of the basin. It must have been partly filled with water a long while ago, which gradually evaporated, leaving its mark in the dust that must have collected there week after week.

"The Frenchman lost his patience at that.

"'My sacred something!' he said. 'Why is the room like this?'

"The same girl who had answered him before, answered him again in the same words. She was standing by the mantel-piece watching us.

"'It is the Count's orders,' she said stolidly.

"'It is by the Count's orders that the bed is not made?' snapped the man.

"'Yes, sir,' said the girl simply.

"Well, that did not content the Frenchman. He exhibited a couple of francs and began to question.

"This is the story that he got out of her. She told it quite simply.

"The last time that Count Jean Marie had come to the place, it had been for his honeymoon. He had come down from Paris with his bride. They had dined together downstairs, very happily and gaily, and had slept in the room in which we were at this moment. A message had been sent out for the carriage early next morning; and the couple had driven away with their trunks, leaving the servants behind. They had not returned, but a message had come from Paris that the house was to be closed. It appeared that the servants who had been left behind had had orders that nothing was to be tidied; even the bed was not to be made; the rooms were to be locked up and left as they were.

"The Frenchman had hardly been able to restrain himself as he heard this unconvincing story; though his wife shook him by the shoulders at each violent gesture that he made, and at the end he had put a torrent of questions.

"'Were they frightened then?'

"'I do not know, sir.'

"'I mean the bride and bridegroom, fool!'

"'I do not know, sir.'

"'Sacred name—and—and—why do you not know?'

"'I have never seen any of them, sir.'

"'Not seen them! Why you said just now—'

"'Yes, sir; but I was not born then. It was thirty years ago.'

"I do not think I have ever seen people so bewildered as we all were. This was entirely unexpected. The Frenchman's jaw dropped; he licked his lips once or twice, and turned away. We all stood perfectly still a moment, and then we went out."

I indulged myself with a pause just here. I was enjoying myself more than I thought I should. I had not told the story for some while, and had forgotten what a good one it was. Besides, it had the advantage of being perfectly true. Then I went on again, with a pleased consciousness of faces turned to me and black-ended cigarettes.

"I must tell you this," I said—"I was relieved to get out of the room. It is sixteen years ago now; and I may have embroidered on my own sensations; but my impression is that I had been just a little uncomfortable even before the girl's story. I don't think that I felt that there was any presence there, or anything of that kind. It was rather the opposite; it was the feeling of an extraordinary emptiness."

"Like a Catholic cathedral in Protestant hands," put in a voice.

I nodded at the zealous, convert-making Father Brent.

"It was very like that," I said, "and had, too, the same kind of pathos and terror that one feels in the presence of a child's dead body. It is unnaturally empty, and yet significant, and one does not quite know what it signifies."

I paused again.

"Well, Reverend Fathers; that is the first Act. We went back to Portrieux: we made inquiries and got no answer. All shrugged their shoulders and said that they did not know.

"There were no tales of the bride's hair turning white in the night, or of any curse or ghost or noises or lights. It was just as I have told you. Then we went back to England, and the curtain came down.

"Now, generally, such curtains have no resurrection. I suppose we have all had fifty experiences of first Acts; and we do not know to this day whether the whole play is a comedy or a tragedy; or even whether the play has been written at all."

"Do not be modern and allusive, Mr. Benson," said Monsignor.

"I beg your pardon, Monsignor; I will not. I forgot myself. Well, here is the second Act. There are only two— and this is a much shorter one.

"Nine years later I was in Paris, staying in the Rue Picot with some Americans. A French friend of theirs was to be married to a man, and I went to the wedding at the Madeleine. It was—well, it was like all other weddings at the Madeleine. No description can be adequate to the appearance of the officiating clergyman and the altar and the bridesmaids and the French gentlemen with polished boots and butterfly ties, and the conversation, and the gaiety, and the general impression of a confectioner's shop and a milliner's and a salon and a holy church. I observed the bride and bridegroom and forgot their names for the twentieth time, and exchanged some remarks in the sacristy with a leader of society who looked like a dissipated priest; with my eyes starting out of my head in my anxiety not to commit a *solécisme* or a *barbarisme*. And then we went home again.

"On the way home we discussed the honeymoon. The pair were going down to a country-house in Brittany. I inquired the name of it; and of course it was the château I had visited nine years before. It had been lent them by Count Jean Marie the Second. The gentleman resided in England, I heard, in order to escape the conscription; he was a connexion of the bride's, and was about thirty years of age.

"Well, of course I was interested, and made inquiries and related my adventure. The Americans were mildly interested too, but not excited. Thirty-nine years is ancient history to that energetic nation." (I bowed to Father Jenks, before I remembered that he was a Canadian; and then pretending that I had not I went on quickly, and missed a dramatic opportunity.) "But two days afterwards they were excited. One of the girls came into *déjeuner*, and said that she had met the bride and bridegroom dining together in the Bois. They had seemed perfectly well, and had saluted her politely. It seemed that they had come back to Paris after one night at the château, exactly as another bride and bridegroom had done thirty-nine years before.

"Before I finish, let me sum up the situation.

"In neither case was there apparently any shocking incident, and yet something had been experienced that broke up plans and sent away immediately from a charming house and country two pairs of persons who had deliberately formed the intention of living there for a while. In both cases the persons in question had come back to Paris.

"I need hardly say that I managed to call with my friends upon the bride and bridegroom; and, at the risk of being impertinent, asked the bride point-blank why they had changed their plans and come back to town.

"She looked at me without a trace of horror in her eyes, and smiled a little.

"'It was *triste*,' she said, 'a little *triste*. We thought we would come away; we desired crowds.'"

I paused again.

"'We desired crowds,'" I repeated. "You remember, Reverend Fathers, that I had experienced a sense of loneliness even with my friends during five minutes spent in that upstairs room. I can only suppose that if I had remained longer I should have experienced such a further degree of that sensation that I should have felt exactly as those two pairs of brides and bridegrooms felt; and have come away immediately. I might even, if I had been in authority, have given orders that nothing was to be touched except my own luggage."

"I do not understand that," said Father Brent, looking puzzled.

"Nor do I altogether," I answered, "but I think I perceive it to be a fact for all that. One might feel that one was an intruder, that one had meddled with something that desired to be left alone, and that one had better not meddle further in any kind of way."

"I suppose you went down there again," observed Monsignor Maxwell.

"I did, a fortnight afterwards. There was only one girl left; the other was married and gone away. She did not remember me; it was nine years ago; and she was a little redder in the face and a little more stolid.

"The lawn had been clipped and mown, but was beginning to grow rank again. Then I went upstairs with her. The room was comparatively clean; there was water in the basin; and clean sheets on the bed; but there was just a little film of dust lying on everything. I pretended I knew nothing and asked questions; and I was told exactly the same story as I had heard nine years before; only this time the date was only a fortnight ago.

"When she had finished, she added:

"'It happened so once before, sir: before I was born.'

"'Do you understand it?' I said.

"'No, sir; the house is a little *triste*, perhaps. Do you think so, sir?'

"I said that perhaps it was. Then I gave her two francs and came away.

"That is all, Reverend Fathers."

There was silence for a minute. Then Padre Bianchi made what I consider a tactless remark.

"Bah! That does not terrify me," he said.

"'Terrify' is certainly not the word," remarked Monsignor Maxwell.

"I am not quite sure about that," ended Father Brent.

The bell rang for night prayers.

"Sum up, Father Rector," said Monsignor without moving. "You have heard all the stories, and Mr. Benson is going tomorrow."

The old priest smiled as he stood up, and was silent for a moment, looking at us all.

"I can only sum up like this with the sentiments with which Monsignor began," he said. "The longer I live and the more I hear and see, the greater I feel my ignorance to be. I heard a man say the other day that Catholics were the only genuine agnostics alive; and that he respected them for it. They knew some things that others did not; but they did not pretend to affirm or to deny that of which they had no possibility of judging. Is that what you meant me to say, Monsignor?"

Monsignor nodded meditatively.

"I think that is a sound conclusion," he said. "I would even go further, and say that the stories that we have heard confirm me, at any rate, in what I said at first. Some of them, if the narrators will forgive me, are so utterly pointless and inexplicable when regarded from the human point of view, that all they seem to prove is that there must be another. Of course we all believe that, but most of us don't act as if we did. It is like looking on at the backs of a crowd; they are attending to something else, not to us at all. Just occasionally we catch the eye of someone who turns round; but that is all."

He drew up his feet suddenly, and leaned forward. Then he went on in a graver voice than it was his custom to use.

"Or, shall we say, each of us is like a new-born child in a great house? In one sense, we are attended to a great deal. All kinds of mysteries are performed of which we are, at least, partly, the object; and what we do know of them, we do know, but that is very little indeed. And meanwhile there are dark corridors along which footsteps pass; we catch the sound of voices, and the glimmer of lights—"

He broke off, and turned to me.

"It is understood, then, Mr. Benson, that if you print these stories, you will add that not one of us commits himself to belief in any of them—except, I suppose, each in his own?"

"I will mention it," I said.

"Perhaps you might say that we do not even commit ourselves to our own. You can say what you like about yours, of course."

"I will mention that, too," I said, "and I will class myself with the rest. The agnostic position is certainly the soundest in all matters outside the Deposit of Faith.... We all stand, then, exactly where we did at the beginning?"

"Certainly I do," said Padre Bianchi.

"We all do," said a number of voices.

Then we went to night prayers, together, for the last time.

THE END

Designed by Fiona Cecile Clarke, the Cluny Media *logo
depicts a monk at work in the scriptorium,
with a cat sitting at his feet.*

*The monk represents our mission to emulate
the invaluable contributions of the monks
of Cluny in preserving the libraries of the West,
our strivings to know and love the truth.*

*The cat at the monk's feet is Pangur Bán, from the
eponymous Irish poem of the 9th century.
The anonymous poet compares his scholarly
pursuit of truth with the cat's happy hunting of mice.
The depiction of Pangur Bán is an homage to the work
of the monks of Irish monasteries and a sign
of the joy we at Cluny take in our trade.*

"Messe ocus Pangur Bán,
cechtar nathar fria saindan:
bíth a menmasam fri seilgg,
mu memna céin im saincheirdd."

Made in the USA
Columbia, SC
23 September 2024

42272420R00124